THE PASSION AND THE MADNESS

THE PASSION AND THE MADNESS

A NOVEL BY
TERRY BUSH

By the Author Crescent Street—2017

ISBN: 978-1-64184-497-0 (Paperback)
      978-1-64184-498-7 (Ebook)

This book is dedicated to the memory of my parents, Kathleen and Leslie.

I'd like to acknowledge and thank
Jill Dawn Morris for her invaluable advice, and
Chris O'Byrne (JETLAUNCH) for his assistance
in arranging the publication of this book.

Terry Bush—October 2020

PROLOGUE

Despite total darkness, a vivid image remains imprinted in my mind. It's the most beautiful picture I've ever seen—but how I wish it never existed.

CHAPTER 1

JULY 1959

"Put your cereal bowl in the sink, then get your shoes on, Sophie, love. It's nearly nine o'clock, so we need to leave in a few minutes or we'll be late," Shirley Weller told her daughter while collecting her shopping basket from the scullery cupboard.

After checking that the front door of the apartment was securely locked, Shirley and her daughter set off on the short walk to the home of Grace and Billy Andrews, a routine they'd followed almost every Saturday morning for the past year. Their journey took them down a steep hill lined on both sides with red brick houses. When they arrived at the High Street, they headed north, passing by a church and several small shops before reaching their destination.

Grace was waiting outside the front door of her terraced home when her guests arrived, where she gave them a typical welcome.

"Good morning ladies. Come on in. William and 'young Shirley' are playing in the backyard if you'd like to join them, Sophie. Billy's up and dressed, ready to watch out for the kids, so we can go shopping whenever you're ready, Shirley."

"No time like the present" Shirley said. "Do you want to walk or take the bus?"

"It looks like we have a warm day ahead of us, so let's stretch our legs and save two pence each in the bargain."

"Sounds good to me, let's go."

Grace had been Shirley's best friend since they were both toddlers, and following the tragic death of Shirley's husband, Grace had made an extra effort for the two of them to spend time together.

On their way to the outdoor market, the two friends caught up on their week's news before Grace asked, "Anything in particular you're looking for today, Shirley?"

"Mainly groceries, but as Sophie has already grown more than an inch this year, I'd like to get her a couple of summer dresses if I can find any at a reasonable price. What about you?"

"A few bits and pieces, and I wouldn't mind new shoes if I see a pair I fancy, though I'll probably wait until Billy takes me into the West End. You get a much better selection there, even if they are more expensive. Billy asked me to pick up fish and chips for him and the kids on our way home. We could stop off and eat ours beforehand if you wish. Or would you sooner get a sandwich from the café?"

"I fancy fish and chips, but maybe we could go to the café for a cup of tea on the way there. Hopefully, we can find a quiet spot, as there's a personal matter I'd like to discuss with you."

Grace stopped in her tracks, and her eyes narrowed. "Is everything all right? It sounds to me like you have a problem."

"Everything is fine, really. It's just that something has cropped up that I'd like your opinion on."

"Shirley, I know you like the back of my hand. I can tell from your tone that something's troubling you. We could go for tea right now, and that way, you can get the matter off your chest."

"Honestly, Grace, it's not like that. Let's wait until we finish our shopping, then I'll tell you all about it."

* * * *

Grace had been antsy from the moment Shirley mentioned her wish to discuss a private matter. She hurried her purchases without the usual browsing and encouraged Shirley to do the same. With their shopping finished Grace led them to the café at close to a marching speed, where she went straight to the counter while Shirley found the only private spot available, a rickety corner table covered with cigarette burns.

"Come on, spit it out," Grace told her friend upon delivering two large mugs of steaming tea. "I'll burst if you keep me waiting another second."

"Let me put your mind at rest. Nothing awful has happened. It's just that I've come across an unusual opportunity, and I'd like to get your take on it."

Shirley gathered her thoughts and was about to explain what had happened when Grace interrupted with a wicked grin on her face.

"I know what it is!" She said louder than intended. "You've met a man. That's nothing to be secretive or embarrassed about. Look, I realize Paul's passing will always be a sad memory for you. That's perfectly normal and understandable. But sometime or other, you have to put things behind you and get on with your life. Billy and I totally understand that. We certainly wouldn't think any less of you if you started seeing another chap. In any case, I suspect that at least initially, you're mainly interested in having a companion."

Shirley put her elbows on the table, placed her head in the palms of her hands, and let out a soft sigh. She'd always appreciated her dear friend's understanding and supportive nature, and while in this instance she'd jumped to the wrong conclusion, she knew it was typical of the way Grace had always looked out for her. "You're half right," she said with a warm smile. "I have met a man. But not one I'm looking to date or start a relationship with."

"What then?" Grace asked, her face taking on a puzzled look.

"Let me back up. Last week, I saw an advertisement in the newspaper. It was for an arts and crafts shop that was looking for a sales assistant. It said the working hours were flexible, and as a bonus, it also offered the successful applicant free use of a fully equipped studio. As you know, I love to paint. I thought it might be worth pursuing even though I have no real experience in that type of work. So on Monday, I phoned the number given. The gentleman who owns the business answered my call and invited me to attend an interview the following day. I met him after work, and the more we talked, the better the job sounded—and, additionally, we seemed to get along really well. I was starting to get quite excited about the prospect until he asked if relocating was a problem. At first, I didn't understand what he meant. When he explained, I realized my mistake. I hadn't taken any notice of the shop's address and assumed it to be local."

"Where on earth is it then?" Grace chimed in.

"It's in the City of Inverness in Scotland."

"What? Okay, now I'm totally confused! Obviously, you can't go to the other end of the world to work. So, what do you want my opinion on?"

"Well, I told him that I hadn't realized where the job was located, and I apologized for wasting his time. I went on to say that even if I wanted to move, being a widow with a young daughter made it impossible for me financially, given I'm only able to make ends meet as a result of local subsidized housing. I thought that would end the discussion, but to my surprise, it didn't. He told me about the living quarters above the shop that Sophie and I could have rent-free if we wanted. He also said there were good schools in the area for children of her age."

"Surely you wouldn't consider moving to another country, Shirley. Plus, it would be nearly impossible for Sophie as she wouldn't know anyone. In any event, why is he looking for someone from around here? That doesn't make any sense!"

"I asked him about that. He told me that he was born and raised in North West London, and his original plan when he opened the business was to give it a 'Southern flavor.' He had hoped to find an appropriate candidate who lived in or around Inverness but was unable to do so. When his last employee quit, he decided to advertise in this area, and he's staying over for a week or so searching for someone to fit the bill."

"I find it hard to believe you're taking this matter seriously. You don't really know anything about the owner or his business, and furthermore, you've never been to that part of the world. It might be a right dump, or worse still, a dangerous place!"

"Everything you say makes perfect sense on the surface. But as I said, we got along extremely well, and I judged him to be a fair and honest man. I raised the same issues as you have. He seemed to understand and addressed them in a logical manner."

"Really? How did he do that? I don't mean to sound rude, but surely there must be other people that fit the bill better than someone with no relevant experience who has never travelled north of Cambridge and, furthermore, has a child in tow!"

"It's a good job. I know you, Grace; otherwise, I could easily take your remarks the wrong way! But yes, I have to agree that on the face of it, you make a fair point. However, he liked the paintings I took to show him. As he told me on the phone, it was important that the successful candidate had an interest in art. And as I've already said, on a personal level, we really seemed to hit it off. He told me that if we reached a point where there was serious interest from both parties, he would pay for Sophie and me to visit the premises without obligation. That would give us the chance to see the area and the living arrangements before making a commitment. Given that the school summer holidays start soon and I can take seven days paid leave, it would give us the chance to check things out. Believe me, I'd never do anything that Sophie wouldn't be happy with. It's true that I have mixed feelings, but all things considered, a fresh start might be good for Sophie and me."

Grace was aware that her friend had been through a difficult time since her personal loss and that perhaps a change of scenery could be helpful. At the same time, she was fearful of Shirley making a big mistake, one she might live to profoundly regret. She knew her friend was sensitive, so she told herself to be gentle while also being clear when giving her opinion. "Look, I understand. But Shirley, you must be very careful. You won't have anyone to look out for you if things go sideways. While Inverness is technically on the same island as London, for all practical purposes, it might as well be on the bloody moon!"

"I know you're only thinking of my best interests, as you've always done," Shirley said softly, brushing away a tear from her cheek. "And I really, really appreciate that. If we were to move, I'd miss you more than I can possibly say. At the same time, apart from you, Billy, and the kids, there's not much keeping me in this area. If our trip is being paid for, I can't see any harm in taking a look. If we're not truly happy with what we see, we'll come straight back, I promise."

Grace leaned across the table and took hold of her friend's hand. "I suppose you're right," she said tenderly. "Mind you, if you do go for a 'look-see', make sure he gives you return tickets in advance—just in case."

Shirley kissed Grace gently on the cheek. "Thank you," she said sweetly.

"Well, apart from the accommodations, have you considered all the other implications of such a move?"

"I've given it some thought. I need to check the local cost of living. I believe it's cheaper than it is here, but I don't know that for certain. Also, I need to ensure it's both safe and easy for Sophie to get back and forth to school and that there are suitable activities to keep her busy. Perhaps my biggest challenge will be giving her the chance to have a say in the matter. I know I'm the parent, and as such, I have to take full responsibility for the decision. I'm not sure how I'll handle it if I like the opportunity, but she's not very keen. If we get to that point, I suppose I'll have to play it by ear. In any event, it's not as though we can't come back in the future if things don't work out, so maybe I'm worrying unnecessarily. What do you think?"

Grace took a deep breath and looked her friend squarely in the eyes. "Quite honestly, Shirley, when you broke your news, my first reaction was to think that you'd gone stark raving bonkers— and I've not really changed my mind about that!" She paused, and her serious expression mellowed. "However, given Paul's passing and the unfortunate relationship you have with his parents, as well as your own come to that, I can see why a fresh beginning has some appeal, at least in theory! I agree you need to make the decision on Sophie's behalf. After all, she's only nine years old, so it would be unfair to place any responsibility on her shoulders. In my opinion, if it becomes clear that she's even the slightest bit unhappy, you should drop the whole idea like a hot potato. Frankly, it all sounds a bit unreal to me, especially as you have a lifelong history of avoiding change where ever possible. But in the final analysis, Shirley, it's up to you. As I've already said, please be extremely careful. Anyway, how did you leave things, and what's supposed to happen next?"

"He said he understood my concerns and wanted me to think it through thoroughly, as he would hate for me to make a decision I might regret later. He suggested that I mull it over during the weekend and call him on Monday. If I'm still interested, we'll meet again on Tuesday and see where we go from there. Of course, this might all end up being a waste of time because I'm sure he's interviewing other candidates, and as you so delicately pointed out, he might well find someone more suitable!"

Grace pulled a face that quickly turned to a loving smile. "If you were to take the plunge, you know I'd miss you tremendously. In spite of that, whatever makes you happy would make me happy as well."

Shirley leaned across the table and hugged her friend tightly. At the conclusion of their embrace, Grace noticed an elderly couple giving them disapproving looks. "I have a feeling those two on the opposite table think we're lesbians," she whispered into her friend's ear.

"Then they can go fuck themselves," Shirley whispered back, an expression Grace had never heard her friend use before and one she was certainly not expecting. The two young ladies were still trying to control their giggling when they eventually arrived back at Grace's home.

CHAPTER 2

Following Shirley's surprising revelation, Grace had convinced herself that nothing more would become of it. She mentioned it to her husband after Shirley and her daughter had departed. "Just a pipe dream," was Billy's reaction. "She's still missing Paul, and she's looking for a way to escape. I don't think moving to Scotland will accomplish that. As we've both said many times before, if she finds another man and a relationship develops, then she may start to move on with her life. The trouble with Shirley is that she never goes out, so how does she expect to meet anyone?"

"I agree. But remember, we introduced her to Paul in the first place, so maybe we should try harder to find her another boyfriend. She's not the most sociable person I've ever met, so if she does end up in Scotland, I doubt she'll ever meet another man. Still, I probably shouldn't be worrying. I think I made it clear, without being too bossy, that I didn't approve. And at the end of the day, Shirley has nearly always taken my advice. I'm almost certain that either her meeting won't take place, or if it does, nothing will come of it. In any event, she's going to stop by at 5:30 on Tuesday afternoon, so we'll get the full scoop then."

*　　*　　*　　*

Grace had just finished making tea when she heard a knock on the front door. "I expect that is Shirley," she told her husband.

"Try not to look pleased when we hear that things didn't work out. She's quite unsure of herself these days, and she's very sensitive, so none of your silly jokes if you don't mind."

Billy feigned a hurt expression. "As if I would!" he exclaimed, throwing his arms in the air and shaking his head from side to side; gestures that Grace responded to by giving her husband the finger while poking out her tongue. Grace felt certain her friend would be upset and had prepared herself to be especially sympathetic, but to her surprise, Shirley's facial expression offered no clues as to what had transpired. "Hello, Shirley. Come on in, love. The tea is brewing," Grace said hesitantly, leading her friend into the sitting room where she asked her husband to 'act as a mother!'

"Thank you," Shirley said. "Mustn't stay too long as I need to get supper ready for Sophie."

Grace made light conversation until Billy returned from the scullery with three cups of tea balanced on a wooden tray. After handing one of them to Shirley and taking a sip from her own, Grace looked gingerly at her friend. She cleared her throat before turning the conversation toward the real reason for the invite. "Well, how did your meeting go today?" She asked cautiously, suspecting that Shirley's brave face would soon disappear and be replaced with tears of disappointment.

"It went pretty well, actually," Shirley said with a thin smile. "Sophie and I will be travelling up to Inverness a week from Friday. We'll be staying there for five days, arriving back on the following Thursday. Mr. Harris, the owner, is making all the arrangements, and I promised him I'd make a final decision within a day or two of us getting back home."

Grace tried to hide her shock, and for what she thought was the first time in her lifelong friendship with Shirley, she found herself at a loss for words. Following a moment of embarrassing silence, she said as earnestly as possible, "I'm pleased to hear that things went well for you, Shirley." Though even she doubted her response sounded sincere.

*   *   *   *

"Well, that's a turn-up for the books," Billy said the moment Shirley took off home. "I'd have bet a week's wages against that happening."

"Just because she's going to check the place out doesn't mean that she'll end up accepting the job. After all, it's a free holiday!" Grace said tersely, slumping back into an armchair and closing her eyes. She was sure that in her heart, she wanted the best for Shirley. But she didn't feel good about what was happening, and to make matters worse, she couldn't figure out why. Something simply didn't seem right! She tried to dissect her thoughts. Was she worried that something bad might happen to her friend? After all, Inverness sounded so remote, and if anything awful did happen, how would she find out about it? Maybe she was feeling selfish and going to miss her friend's company if she did end up accepting the job? *Could I possibly even be a little jealous?* She asked herself. That didn't seem logical as such a move had no appeal to her whatsoever. Even more puzzling was that Shirley had never been adventurous or outgoing. Perhaps, she simply couldn't relate to the mindset of a woman who'd found herself a widow at a young age. Despite chewing over every angle that she could think of, Grace couldn't find a convincing rationalization for her unsettled feelings. She found herself frustrated, particularly as she'd always played the role of a big sister to Shirley, providing advice and direction on many issues concerning her well-being. *Why then*, she asked herself, *was she not able to do so on this occasion?* Maybe things would be clearer in the morning, she concluded, before telling Billy she was going to bed early in order to get a good night's sleep.

*   *   *   *

The following Friday, Grace accompanied Shirley and Sophie on the bus ride to the South Harrow underground station in order to wish them farewell for their long journey north. The first leg would be by 'tube' to Kings Cross station. There, they'd catch the mainline train to Inverness. Mr. Harris had made dinner reservations in the dining carriage and booked a 'sleeper compartment' so they could enjoy a comfortable night's rest. He would be meeting them at Inverness station on Saturday morning and driving them from there to his shop.

When they arrived at the ticket counter, Grace said, "Both of you take good care and have a safe journey. Look out for your mum, Sophie, and don't talk to strangers!" before kissing Sophie on the cheek and giving Shirley a huge hug.

"Thanks so much, Grace," Shirley said. "We really appreciate you seeing us off. We'll be back next Thursday, and I'll stop by as soon as I get organized to let you know how things went."

"I look forward to it. Why don't you come around as usual on Saturday morning? We can go shopping and chat over a cup of tea." Grace called out.

"That would be smashing," Shirley called back while handing their tickets to the collector at the entry turnstile. All three of them were still waving their hands vigorously as Shirley and Sophie disappeared up the escalator leading to the departure platform.

*   *   *   *

Grace spent much of the following week talking aimlessly and repeatedly about Shirley's visit to Inverness. Even Billy, who typically avoided confrontation with his wife, found himself saying, "For Christ's sake, give it a rest, sweetheart. You're starting to get on my nerves. You've said yourself that she'll probably back out when push comes to shove. In any event, you only have to wait until Saturday to get the answer, so please stop obsessing over nothing." While deep down inside, Grace knew Billy was right, his comments did not improve her frame of mind; in fact, it felt the opposite. In a fleeting moment of anger, she shouted aloud, "Men! Your lot will never understand these types of things! And you in particular, Billy, you don't have a clue. It's obvious that you couldn't care less about my feelings. You showed more interest when Arsenal's goalkeeper got injured than you have in my best friend's situation!"

Billy had learned over the years to steer clear of further conversation on the odd occasion his wife behaved in a way that he secretly described as "one of her crazy hormonal outbursts." Experience had taught him that no matter how he reacted or what he said, it would likely be taken the wrong way. He believed that the best course of action was to simply put some space between him and his wife until her mood improved. "I think I'll pop down to the pub for a quick pint," he said while putting on his coat and setting off without waiting for a response.

"Typical! That's it, just piss off out! No doubt you have more in common with your drunken friends than you have with your wife," were the last words Billy heard Grace scream as she slammed the front door behind him.

*　*　*　*

Grace hadn't been able to sleep well on Friday night. In spite of knowing that she'd get Shirley's news the following morning, she continued to agonize over the possible outcome. Though having pretty much convinced herself that Shirley couldn't possibly go through with the move, a grain of doubt still lingered. Normally, she stayed in bed until 7:30 on Saturdays, but shortly after 6 o'clock, she was up cooking breakfast. Billy was inwardly annoyed at being woken early on a weekend, but in the circumstances, he knew better than to show it. Only a few more hours, he told himself, and then, hopefully, his wife would be able to put an end to a week of senseless fretting.

*   *   *   *

Grace was standing within arm's reach of her front door when Shirley knocked on it shortly after 9 o'clock. Realizing it may give the wrong impression if she opened it immediately, Grace waited for a few moments before doing so. "Hello Shirley, hello Sophie, welcome back," she said, giving both of her visitors a hug before leading them inside. Earlier, she had told herself to relax and allow Shirley the opportunity to talk about her trip when she was good and ready. But the minute her guests arrived, Grace found her anxiety returning, and she couldn't prevent herself from suggesting they take off on their shopping trip the moment Sophie removed her coat. Keen to avoid possible tension arising, Billy said, "Good idea, love. That will give you more time to look around, and I'm sure you both have lots to talk about, so you'll probably want to have lunch together. I'll take the kids out for pie and mash, so you don't need to hurry home."

On leaving the house, Grace renewed the promise that she'd made to herself earlier, but they'd barely turned the first corner on their fifteen-minute walk to the market when her self-control vanished into thin air. "Let's stop at the café on our way, Shirley," she said abruptly.

"But haven't you just had breakfast? Perhaps we should wait until lunch time."

"Look, Shirley, let me be blunt! I've been waiting all damn week to find out how your trip went, and, more importantly, if you've decided to take the job or not. If you keep me in the dark any longer, I might just blow my stack!"

"Sorry, Grace, I wasn't trying to string you along, honestly. I just thought we'd discuss it over lunch, but of course, we can stop at the café and talk now if that's what you prefer."

✳   ✳   ✳   ✳

"Right, I'm all ears," Grace said when she placed two mugs of tea on the corner table Shirley had found.

Shirley hadn't gotten any further than describing the sleeper car when Grace brusquely interrupted. "Look, I'm interested to hear all the details later. But kindly tell me this minute, have you accepted the bloody job or not?"

Shirley took a sip of tea, clasped her hands together, and slowly leaned back in her chair. "I have," she said softly. "I telephoned Mr. Harris yesterday afternoon with my decision. I've got to give two weeks' notice at my current job, and I need some time to pack. Mr. Harris has agreed to pay for the transportation of our furniture and belongings. We'll arrive in Inverness the middle of August. That will allow us to get Sophie settled and enrolled at school before the new term begins."

"Well, that's good," Grace mumbled, apparently unaware her mouth was hanging open.

CHAPTER 3

Grace had been impatiently checking the postman's daily deliveries for more than a month. She knew that Shirley would have many pressing priorities in her new situation, but the absence of a letter following her friend's assuring words, "I'll write as soon as possible, I promise," was beginning to irk her.

That Friday, however, her growing irritation quickly turned to elation when she saw the postmark on the envelope that had just been dropped through her letterbox. She picked it up and ran to her bedroom, wanting to read it in private.

4th of October 1959

Dear Grace,

I'm sorry it's taken me so long to write this letter. Things have been hectic since we arrived here.

Initially, my main concerns focused around Sophie. I was really worried whether or not she would adapt to the changes our move entailed. Fingers crossed, it's gone quite well so far. She likes her new teacher, and she's already made a couple of friends. You'll have a hard time believing this, Grace, but she's already starting to get a hint of a Scottish accent! I don't think that will ever happen with me, as I can't imitate the locals even if I try.

I'm thrilled with our new home. As you know, I quite liked it when we came for our first look. But Mr. Harris made a number of improve-

ments between then and our subsequent move. I now have a new cooker and, get this, a fridge! He's also hung a number of paintings on the walls, which makes it feel more comfortable.

The job is going well. It took me a couple of weeks to learn where everything was kept. But now that I'm familiar with all of our products, it allows me to handle things on my own when needs be. That really helps, as it gives Mr. Harris the freedom to come and go when he has other things to do.

I think you'd like the local area. It's very pretty, lots of trees and vegetation everywhere. The town of Inverness also seems nice, at least the little bit we've seen of it. We haven't had the opportunity to explore much yet, but we plan on doing so now that our flat is organized.

Well, that's about it for now. Please write as soon as you can.

With all my love, Shirley (and Sophie)

✳   ✳   ✳   ✳

28th of October 1959

Dear Shirley,

It was nice to hear from you (at long last!). I'm pleased things seem to be working out well.

I didn't realize how long it's been since I'd written a letter. I had to borrow the paper I'm writing on from my mum.

It's hard to imagine Sophie having a Scottish accent. It probably makes you laugh, I would think! Do the schools teach the same subjects as they do here in Harrow?

All's well with the family. It's difficult to believe William will turn ten in a couple of months from now. Where does the time go? Young Shirley is doing fine. Though she doesn't turn four until January, she's already starting to read.

Billy sends his love. He cut his hand at work last week and had to have five stitches. Still, as long as Arsenal keeps winning, I don't think he'd mind much if his arm fell off!

I've been busy knitting sweaters for the kids. With winter coming, I had them try on the ones I made last year, and they're already too tight. William continues to grow like a weed. He's going to be tall like his dad.

Last weekend, the kids and I spent several hours gathering wood for the bonfire in the park as it's Guy Fawkes' day next week. Is that celebrated in Scotland? Before we know it, Christmas will be here! It just occurred to me that this will be your first Christmas away from home. Do you have any plans to celebrate?

Before I forget, I bumped into Paul's mum last week. She told me that the council had dropped off a couple of boxes that, apparently, you'd left behind when you took off to Inverness. As far as she knows, they're full of paper files and books. Possibly things you no longer want, but if you do, I suggest you let her know so she can forward them to you.

Well, that's all for now. Don't take so long in writing to me next time—just kidding!

Love, Grace.

P.S. By the way, PLEASE don't forget that we agreed not to exchange Christmas presents this year, especially given the outrageous cost of mailing a parcel!

*　*　*　*

27th of November 1959

Dear Grace,

I'm writing this letter in front of a huge coal fire. The weather has suddenly turned cold, and we have to bundle up when we go outside. It hasn't snowed in Inverness yet, but it has in the hills, which are just a few miles away. I took Sophie there last weekend with one of her school friends, and they built a snowman.

Sophie is really taking to the area. I think a lot of it has to do with her school, which she loves. She told me the other day that she never wants to go back to Harrow, as she thinks Inverness is a much better place to live. I must say that in some ways, it made me think hard. Don't get me wrong, I'm enjoying it here as well, especially the job (more about that in a minute), but I suppose it occurred to me that if I ever wanted to go back to Harrow, I more than likely would meet resistance from Sophie! It's funny how things can turn around in ways that you don't see coming.

Grace, the job is turning out to be better than I could have ever possibly imagined. I love helping customers pick the products that best match their needs. Having never dealt with the public in my previous employment, I didn't get the chance to see how rewarding it is to help others. This is especially true when people make return visits and thank me for recommending items that worked well for them. It's very satisfying.

In addition to the work, I've started using the art studio. It's a beautiful room, appropriately decorated and equipped with everything one could wish for. Mr. Harris has also been helpful in that regard. He's shown me several techniques that have improved my handy work. He's also pretty talented himself. He paints regularly, and we sell some of his work in the shop.

I'm told December is a busy month for us, and in addition to my work, I've got to spend some evenings at the school. Sophie is rehearsing for a show that the kids put on at this time of the year, and I'm keen to watch. Somehow, over the next couple of weekends, I've got to find time to squeeze Christmas shopping into my schedule; although, I suppose I don't really have that much to buy. Sophie and I will probably celebrate Christmas day on our own, but I will be cooking a small turkey, so we'll have fun together. I don't think I'll have time to write again until the New Year, so our best to you all, and have a wonderful and safe time over the holidays.

Love, Shirley.

* * * *

19th February 1960

Dear Shirley,

I trust you are keeping well, and I hope my card arrived safely. I had planned on writing sooner but something unexpected cropped up that's changed everything. I hope you're sitting down when you read what I have to say next. I'm pregnant again! I must be honest; it wasn't planned. Billy wasn't too happy when I told him. "How the hell did that happen?" was his initial reaction. You can imagine how I replied to that! He's got somewhat used to the idea now, and I'm sure we'll both be thrilled when the baby arrives. But it's going to set back our plans, as I was hoping to start a part time job when young Shirley gets settled into school. Oh well, nothing we can do about it now though it will put a strain on our finances and obviously limit the things we can afford to do.

Well, that's probably more than enough news for one letter!
I look forward to hearing from you when you have the time.
Love, Grace.
P.S. Is there any chance you'll come back for a visit this year?

* * * *

30th of March 1960

Dear Grace,

I must say that I was truly taken back by your news; though personally, I think it's wonderful. In the long run, I bet you and Billy will be pleased that you had three children. I realize that it will be harder to make ends meet, but at the end of the day, family is far more important than money.

Things here continue to go well. January and February were really cold, but in a way both Sophie and I quite like the weather. It's actually exhilarating. Sophie is now playing the violin and practicing for the school orchestra. Also, she joins me in the art studio most Saturdays, and Mr. Harris has been helping her as well.

Talking of Mr. Harris, he invited Sophie and me for tea at his home last weekend. We had a pleasant time, and we got to meet his daughter, which came as a shock because he'd never mentioned her before. While he and I get along well, we seldom talk about personal matters, and I don't like to pry. My guess is that he is either divorced, or perhaps, his wife died. Actually, the latter doesn't seem likely to me, as I can't see any reason why he wouldn't have mentioned it. Anyway, there's no point in speculating. Given the amount of time we spend together at the shop, I'd imagine he'll tell me more about himself when he feels comfortable doing so.

With regard to your question about my making a trip back to Harrow. Frankly, I hadn't given it any real thought until you raised the subject. Now that I have, the answer, unfortunately, is almost certainly no. Naturally, I'd love to visit you and the family, but I just don't see it happening for a number of reasons. First of all, summertime is when we get more tourists in the area, so I'll be really busy at the shop. Second, Sophie has several things lined up including a camping and hiking trip that the school is arranging. And third, a bit like you I suppose, there's the question of money. While I'm happy with what Mr. Harris pays me, it's not a lot, and with Sophie growing up, my expenses are increasing as well. I think I may get a wage rise when I finish my first year, but I'm not overly optimistic that will amount to much. As I've already said, Mr. Harris is a fair and honest man. However, as I've slowly learned about the business, I don't think there's much profit in it at the end of the day. There's plenty of competition, and most people who draw and paint do so as a hobby, not a business. Consequently, they spend as little as they can get away with.

There is of course another issue regarding a possible trip home. Where would we stay? I don't think I could stand spending a week or two with my parents, and in all probability, they'd most likely find some reason why it wasn't possible. There's no way we could afford a boarding house or hotel, so short of camping on Harrow common, a visit is not realistic.

My dear friend, I sincerely hope everything works out well for you and your family. I'm sure that God intends for us to meet up some time or other, and I truly look forward to that day.
Love Shirley.

*   *   *   *

7th of June 1960

Dear Shirley,
I know it's been a while, and I apologize for taking so long to write. It's not a very good excuse really, but I wasn't very well for a while. I never had morning sickness with the other two, but the third time is unlucky I suppose.
I've been a bit better the last week or so. So hopefully, that stage is behind me. I'm really starting to show! My mum told me that your stomach muscles lose strength after a couple of pregnancies, so I've a feeling I'm going to look like a beached whale by the time this one arrives.
The good news is that Billy has gotten more enthusiastic about being a dad again. Strictly between you and me, there might be another reason for his more cheerful mood. I don't think I've ever told you this before, but when I was pregnant with young Shirley, I wasn't particularly receptive in the bedroom. For some reason, and I honestly don't know what it is, that hasn't happened this time around!
William starts secondary school in September. Next thing we'll know, he'll be off to work! Young Shirley continues to do well. In addition to reading, she now likes painting, so she not only bears your name but also I think she's following in your footsteps!
Time for me to sign off as Billy will be home soon, and I need to get dinner started.
Love, Grace.

*   *   *   *

22nd of August 1960

Dear Grace,

It's hard to believe we've been here for a whole year! Where has the time gone? Only another 2 weeks and Sophie will be back at school. Summer has flown by, maybe because I've been so busy at work.

Sophie is starting to change from a little girl into a young woman. When I think back on it, she's light years ahead of where I was at her age. In some ways, it makes me feel especially proud; though in others, it gives me a certain amount of anxiety. I'm pretty sure you know what I mean by that, though it's difficult to elaborate in writing. That being said, I'm confident she's a smart, young lady who won't do anything silly.

Changing subjects, and on a very unfortunate note, the other day Mr. Harris told me that his daughter was planning a short stay with her aunt next month. He has decided to use the break as an opportunity to visit a friend who lives on the Isle of Skye, so he asked if Sophie and I would like to join him. His friend has a vacation cottage where the three of us could stay. It so happens that his plan coincides with a weekend where Sophie has arranged a sleepover with two of her school friends, so she wouldn't be able to go. I suppose I hadn't thought things through properly; as following my initial grateful acceptance , it occurred to me that not only would I be going away with just Mr. Harris, but we'd also be staying in the same home. Regrettably, I made a hash of trying to explain why, on reflection, I thought it may not be such a good idea after all, and then of course, I realized that I was more or less saying that I didn't trust him! I didn't need to look in a mirror to know my face had turned bright red, and I can hardly remember feeling so embarrassed in my entire life. Being the gentleman that he is, Mr. Harris quickly recognized my dis-comfort and obviously the reason for it. He apologized, saying he should have been more tactful before asking. Naturally, I appreciated his sensitive response, but when I thought about it further, I realized he'd made it per-fectly clear there were three bedrooms in the cottage and that he'd assumed Sophie would be coming with me. Not knowing what to say or do next, the conversation ended awkwardly with me making up some lame excuse of needing to run a few errands. And as you might guess, I only just made it out of the room before bursting into tears.

I've been agonizing over the matter ever since, and though I haven't yet detected any difference in his attitude towards me, I'm concerned that I may have caused an unspoken rift.

Perhaps I'm overreacting, but I feel I may have permanently damaged a relationship that had been steadily growing over the last year with a man I respect greatly. My emotions on the subject have been all over the place, and frankly, I'm quite unsure what to do next.

I've considered resigning my position and coming back to Harrow for fear that things with Mr. Harris will never be the same again. At the other end of the spectrum, I've thought about apologizing for my behavior and hoping time will heal any wounds that I've inflicted. To make matters worse, I also have to consider how any decision I make might affect Sophie, particularly as she is very happy living here.

I can't tell you how much I wish I was able to discuss all of the above with you in person. You've always been a shoulder for me to lean on, and I think I appreciate that more now than I ever did in the past

In the circumstances, however, this is something I must decide for myself. I can only pray I do the right thing.

With all my love,

Shirley.

*   *   *   *

3rd of September 1960

Dear Shirley,

I was very concerned to hear about the troubles you are experiencing in your relationship with Mr. Harris. No doubt by now you will have made your decision, and I hope with all my heart things turn out for the best. Please give me an update as soon as you possibly can.

I hope you'll understand that in my current circumstances this will be a very short letter. I just wanted you to know what was happening at this end. Yesterday, I had a visit from the midwife. We're expecting things to go smoothly, and it looks like the baby will be arriving in the next couple of weeks. The kids and Billy are all well. Billy is trying hard to do his best though occasionally I think he lives on a different emotional planet. I probably never will totally understand him; although, I don't doubt that in the bottom of his heart he really cares about me.

Love from us all (and from the little one due to arrive soon).

P.S. I promise to write as soon as I'm up and about again.

*　*　*　*

10th of October 1960

Dear Grace,

I do hope everything went well with the birth of your baby, whom I assume has arrived by now. I can't wait to get the details, but I know you must be very busy and that I will hear from you when you able to get around to it.

I'm thrilled to tell you that I have wonderful news regarding Mr. Harris. After thinking things through, I decided that the only proper thing to do was to tell him the absolute truth and see how things progressed from there. Luckily, I was able to meet with him in the privacy of our flat after work, as Sophie had orchestra practice that evening. I apologized without making any excuses, saying that it must have sounded as if I didn't trust him. I gave him my absolute assurance that wasn't the case, in fact, just the opposite. I was dreading his response, but he simply smiled and said he totally understood. I was extremely relieved to hear that but wasn't expecting what came next. "In that case Shirley," he said, "I can't see any reason for you not to join me. I'm sure you'll enjoy the scenery, and I'm quite certain you'll get along well with my friend."

He couldn't have been more accurate. We had an absolutely wonderful time. He's such an interesting man and very considerate. I'm a little embarrassed to say this, but when he dropped me off back home, he kissed me for the first time. It was only a quick peck on the cheek, but it made me feel a lot closer to him than ever before. To be perfectly honest, I think I'm falling for him a little bit, but at the same time, I'm fighting against it, mainly because it doesn't make a lot of sense. Perhaps I'm just protecting myself against getting hurt, as it's hard to believe it could develop into anything of a romantic nature. Oh well, I expect I'll get over any delusions I might be experiencing.

Please write as soon as you feel up to it.

Lots of love, from Shirley

∗　∗　∗　∗

1st of December 1960

Dear Shirley,

David Andrews entered this world on September 28th. He's a bundle of joy, weighing in at just over 8 pounds; although despite his size, it was a relatively quick and easy delivery.

Billy is happy, as he thinks he has yet another Arsenal supporter in the making! You know Shirley, I've sometimes been a little critical of Billy in the past, but now, I have a completely different perspective. Having a third child with two others to look out for has its challenges, and as my mum is getting older, I've not had much help from her this time around. Billy, on the other hand, has really stepped up. He's up early to make the kids breakfast and get them ready for school. Then he works as much overtime as he can because he knows our expenses have increased. When he gets home, he helps out with the laundry and other household chores--- without complaining, I might add! Admittedly, he doesn't always do things the same way as I would, but I now realize that's really not the point. What is important is that when push comes to shove, Billy is always there for me and the family. God love him.

Changing gears, I'm really interested to hear more about you and Mr. Harris. I must admit it never occurred to me that the two of you might ever have anything other than a professional relationship, but reading between the lines, maybe I was wrong!

Can't wait to hear what's going on at your end.

Love Grace.

*   *   *   *

22nd of January 1961

Dear Grace,

We had a fantastic Christmas and New Year, and I hope you did too.

Sophie is still reveling in her life here, and that alone makes everything good for me.

For my part, on a personal level that is, things seem to only be getting better. For starters, I no longer call Mr. Harris, Mr. Harris. I now call him James! It might be an exaggeration to say we occasionally go on dates, but often when our respective daughters are busy, we go out for supper or a walk. Last weekend, he took me to the cinema. Guess what? During the second film, we held hands!

I keep telling myself to remain calm and not build up false hopes, but in all honesty Grace, I'm pretty sure I'm in love with James. Being close to him makes me happy. It's hard to tell how he feels about me. I'm fairly certain that he enjoys my company, and in his own way, he's told me as such. Whether it goes beyond that, or if it ever will, is difficult to say. I suppose I will simply have to wait and see. In the meantime, I'm happier than I've been for a long, long while.

I know you must be very busy, but please write when you get the chance.

All my love,

Shirley.

*   *   *   *

12th of March 1961

Dear Shirley,

It warmed my heart to hear how happy you are at long last. You deserve it. David is getting bigger by the week, and he's a joy to have around despite the extra washing that he creates. William and young Shirley are doing well, and Billy got a pay rise last month, which helps out a bit. So all in all, I've no complaints.

My mother came down with a serious bout of flu a few weeks ago, and I must say I was worried about her. Fortunately, she's much better now, though it was another reminder to me that she's getting older. Dad seems to plod along without any health issues (as far as I know), though he's not one to complain and likely wouldn't tell me if he had any.

On the health front, I'm doing fine; although I've not yet lost the weight I'd hoped to since David arrived. I get plenty of exercise just taking care of the house and the family, but I find myself snacking at all times of the day and sometimes well into the night! To make matters worse, I'm not eating healthy, rather, devouring anything sweet or with butter on it. Don't remember doing this last time around. I really need to get a grip or else I'll soon be mistaken for a barrage balloon! And on a purely practical matter, all of my clothes are so tight I feel like I've been mummified. No use complaining though, as I'm the only one who can do something about it, and I've promised myself to get on a better routine starting this weekend.

That's about it for now. I sincerely hope we can meet up one of these days, though I know it doesn't appear likely in the foreseeable future.

Take good care and please write when you have the time.

Love,

Grace.

*   *   *   *

16th of May 1961

Dear Grace,

I trust all is well on your end.

You might want to make yourself a cup of strong tea and take a seat in a comfortable chair before you read any further. I'll give you five minutes to do so...

Do you have your tea ready yet? Okay, if not, I did warn you!

As I mentioned in my last letter, James and I had started what one might call friend style dating. We have been having pleasant conversations, holding hands when out of sight from others, and shared that odd goodnight kiss, though one could hardly have described that as an act of great passion. A couple of weekends ago, when both of our daughters were away on school related activities, I invited James to have dinner with me in our flat. I went out of my way to cook him the best meal I could think of, and I even splashed out and bought a bottle of red wine as I knew he was partial to a glass or two.

You know me, I spent the entire afternoon worrying myself silly that I'd mess something up, but luckily when the time came, I was able to serve a pretty respectable dinner, which put me at ease. So much so, that I also had a glass of wine, which pleased James, as I knew he preferred not to drink alone.

When I'd finished clearing up, which James helped me with, I made coffee that we drank while sitting together on the sofa. James brought a small flask of whiskey with him, which he likes as an after-dinner drink. He offered me a small nip, which I politely refused though eventually, at his insistence, I gave it a go. It made me shudder right down to my toes, which made him laugh almost uncontrollably, and I soon found myself doing the same. I've heard it said that laughter is the spice of life, though I never took that expression seriously before. But now I most certainly do! The incident seemed to change everything. Our conversation went in a different direction, and in short order, we touched on subjects that we'd never discussed beforehand. The evening went by rapidly, and before I knew it, the clock chimed eleven times. Five hours has never passed so quickly, and I was praying it would slow down, thinking it very unlikely James would stay beyond midnight.

Just when I sensed James was about to take his leave, he turned toward me and smiled sweetly. What happened next I can only describe as something I would imagine is nearly every girl's romantic fantasy come true. He took me in his arms, hugged me tightly, and kissed me in a way that I've never been kissed before. It all seemed magical. I was floating on air, and I hoped beyond all hopes that the moment would never end. We were still kissing zealously when he put one arm around my shoulders and the other under my hips in order to lift me up. By now, I'd entered a twilight zone, and the next thing I became fully conscious of was that we were in bed making love!

I hope you won't think the worst of me for what must sound like behavior totally unbefitting a lady, but Grace, I can only tell you that in the moment it all felt so right. We didn't sleep much that night, but when morning came around, I was still in a state of euphoria, and it was clear James felt the same way. As the girls were not due back till later in the afternoon, we had plenty of time to discuss what was happening between us. Shortly after the clock chimed eleven for the second time since James had arrived, he proposed marriage! And as you might have guessed by now, it took me less than eleven seconds to accept! I'm so wonderfully happy, Grace; I don't have the words to describe it.

We've decided against a church wedding, and instead, we plan on visiting Gretna Green in a fortnight's time to complete our vows.

The news gets even better. We had some apprehension in telling our respective daughters of our decision. To our great joy, they greeted the situation with unconditional acceptance. It helps no end that they get along well together, and I'm optimistic that we will have a happy blended family.

So, did you make yourself tea? I hope that I didn't make you spill it or pass out on your chair!

Naturally, I'll write soon after our wedding. We're going to delay our honeymoon until the summer, and we'll be taking the girls along with us. They both think that's a bit of a hoot, but I'm sure we will all have fun. Love and kisses from your devoted friend, Shirley.

CHAPTER 4

"I do," James said, beaming into the dark brown eyes of the woman he'd grown to adore.

"Now, kindly place this gold band on Shirley's finger as a symbol of your everlasting love," the officiating administrator said, moments prior to proclaiming, "James and Shirley Harris, you are now husband and wife. James, would you like to kiss your bride?" A question that James privately thought to be unnecessary!

At the conclusion of the short but poignant Gretna Green ceremony, the newlyweds, together with their two daughters, celebrated with a three-course luncheon in the local hotel restaurant.

*   *   *   *

On their return to Inverness, Shirley and Sophie moved into the cottage where James had previously lived with his daughter, Daphne, thereby finally uniting the families as one. While the marriage ceremony had been an important occasion for all, the delayed honeymoon was clearly the icing on the cake. And given that the girls were going to accompany their parents on this rather unusual vacation, they were keen to know more about the plans.

"Well, next week marks the end of the school term, girls. Your mother and I have decided that we'll start our fortnight's vacation the following week. And given that we've foolishly agreed to drag you two rascals along with us, we thought we'd at least let you have some say in putting together our itinerary," James said, pulling a funny face while staring at his bloodline daughter. Daphne had long appreciated her dad's offbeat humor, which Sophie had tuned into as well.

"Thanks a bunch, Dad," Daphne said when she gained control of her contagious giggling fit. "But seriously, we appreciate you and mum listening to us—even if it does go in one ear and out the other." It was a comeback line that tested James' ability to prevent himself from laughing. "Given a choice, Sophie, what would you like to do on our vacation?" Daphne asked, reverting to a more serious tone.

"Though I've been living here for nearly two years," Sophie started out, "apart from our school trip to Edinburgh, I've never been far from Inverness. My geography teacher told us there are numerous beautiful and interesting sights to see in Scotland, many of which have a fascinating history. So, I'd be in favor of travelling as much as possible rather than staying in one place."

"I like that idea, Sophie," Daphne chimed in. "While I've been here much longer than you, I really haven't seen a great deal of the country either." The two girls turned to their respective parents, who looked expectantly at each other.

Shirley reacted first. "Some travelling appeals to me, but maybe Dad wants to get some rest, especially given the busy time he's had recently. Actually, I'm happy one way or the other, so James, what do you think? Do you like the idea of travelling?"

James had adopted a solemn disposition, but slowly his face lit up. "Like the idea? I bloody love the idea!" He shouted while breaking into a wild Scottish jig that neither Shirley nor Sophie had seen him perform before.

Having reached a consensus on the basic plan for their vacation, the family spent much of the following days working out the details, which included travel routes, meals, sightseeing, and overnight accommodation arrangements. Shirley and James were so invigorated by their daughters' ideas that they privately agreed the trip sounded like it might be even more fun than if they were going away alone!

*   *   *   *

In the early morning of August 1st, the Harris family ate a hearty breakfast, and by seven o'clock, they'd loaded their station wagon and were on their way. Leaving Inverness, they headed east, following the coastline until they reached Elgin, where they stopped for a picnic lunch. In the afternoon, they continued cross country, arriving at the guest house in Aberdeen where they'd spent the night. The following day was largely devoted to sightseeing, and they managed to visit St. Machar's Cathedral, Kings College, the Aberdeen Art Gallery, and the Maritime Museum before it became time to drive five miles south and check into the camping site where they'd reserved a spot for the night

With their tent erected and the cooking equipment set up, Daphne said, "Mum, Dad—Sophie and I have a great idea! Why don't you two take a nap while we make dinner?"

"Not sure I fancy burnt offerings tonight!" James replied jovially.

"We might surprise you," Sophie chimed in

"I'm certain you will, but I was looking forward to waking up in the morning without a stomach ache!" James said in mocking humor.

"I think you're pushing your luck," Shirley told her husband, giggling at the sight of Daphne pretending to threaten her father with a bottle of cold water.

"Okay, I surrender!" James shouted. "Your mother and I will take a nap while you girls do your thing. My only request is that you wake us immediately if you happen to set the tent on fire!"

Amused by their father's ongoing banter, but wishing to demonstrate their culinary skills, the girls set about preparing dinner, and thirty minutes later, they served up a presentable meal consisting of scrambled eggs, sausages, and baked beans.

"I've tasted worse," James said after heartily swallowing the last mouthful on his plate, "It's just that I don't remember when!"

Before darkness fell, the four campers were happily snuggled up in their sleeping bags despite that the back of James' tee shirt was still soaking wet.

*　　*　　*　　*

The balance of their vacation took the Harrises south through Edinburgh, before circling in an anticlockwise direction, finally arriving back home late on a Friday evening. In addition to seeing many amazing and fascinating sights, they were blessed with fine weather conditions throughout, leaving the entire family with a wonderful memory that they'd treasure for many years to come.

*　　*　　*　　*

Following their extraordinary family honeymoon, Shirley and James quickly settled into a lifestyle that they found to be nothing short of sheer heaven on Earth. They loved working together in the shop, and while only producing a modest profit, it afforded them everything they truly wanted. The girls continued to do well at school, and both pursued healthy and interesting pastimes. Sophie devoted most of her free time to painting in the studio with her parents, as well as participating in the school orchestra. Daphne, on the other hand, focused more on outdoor activities and sports. Though the girls' interests varied, their friendship continued to grow, providing much satisfaction to their parents, who saw a bright future ahead for both of them.

After the Easter break, Daphne ramped up her studies for the upcoming CGC exams. It was important that she do well as this was the first major step towards the university education she hoped to pursue. While she was still vacillating between a career in human medicine or as a veterinarian, it was necessary that she secure a degree for either pursuit.

Sophie also had exams coming up at the same time as her stepsister. Recognizing the effort their children were putting in, James and Shirley signed both of their daughters up for an end of term school getaway trip as a reward.

Finally, to everyone's relief, exams were over, and to James and Shirley's delight, their daughters were both confident that they'd done well. The following Friday, Sophie and Daphne packed their cases in preparation for their school trip, and at eight-thirty the next morning, the girls kissed their mother goodbye.

"Have a great time the both of you," Shirley said, giving Sophie a final hug. "Remember to keep a diary and take photographs, as I want to know everything about your trip when you get back."

When the two girls climbed into the back seat of the family car, James kissed his wife. "I'll drop the girls off first, but when I get back, let's drive into town and have lunch at the steak house that's just opened. And tomorrow we can drive to the beach for a picnic."

"That sounds like a lot of fun, darling. I'm going to miss the girls, of course, but at the same time, it gives us an opportunity to spend more time together."

When her husband and children departed, Shirley set about the week's laundry. If she and James were going to enjoy the balance of the weekend, she needed to finish her chores quickly, especially as she disliked ironing on Sundays.

Engrossed in her housework, Shirley lost track of time. On hearing a knock on the front door, she glanced at the clock and was surprised to find that James had been gone for nearly two hours. She smiled to herself, thinking that most likely, he'd spent an inordinate amount of time briefing the girls on the dos and don'ts for their trip. Not only that but in his excitement, it appeared that he'd also managed to forget his door key!

When Shirley opened the front door, she was ready to make fun of her husband and his forgetfulness, but to her surprise, it was not James standing there. Rather, it was Stuart McFarland. Stuart was a local resident, an occasional customer at the shop, and the local police constable.

"Good morning, Stuart. Sorry if I looked a little startled. I thought it was James and that he'd forgotten his key. How can I help you?"

At first, it appeared as if Constable McFarland was fascinated with Shirley's shoes until he lifted his head and looked her square in the eyes. "Mrs. Harris," he started out, addressing her in a formal way that Shirley couldn't remember him doing before, "I have a warrant for your arrest."

CHAPTER 5

I was born in Harrow, Middlesex, on July 16th, 1931, and our family home was a two-bedroom rented apartment. Four weeks after my birth, I was christened Shirley Anne Vickers.

One of my earliest memories is playing with a girl who lived a few doors away. Her name was Grace, and she would become my best friend. I started school at five years of age, and as Grace was only one month older than me, we ended up in the same class. When I look back, I suppose our relationship was an unlikely one. Apart from the close proximity of our homes, we were different in almost every other way. While I was shy and lacked self-confidence, she was outgoing and sure of herself. In addition to our personality differences, our interests varied as well, but despite these factors, we were always close and comfortable together. I think that maybe Grace enjoyed cheering me up, which was something that, unfortunately, I often needed, and perhaps I played the role of the little sister she wanted to take care of.

I was eight years old when World War Two began. Though the conflict had dramatic consequences for many families, mine seemed to be able to ignore its existence. Even when I got older, I never did find out why my father wasn't required to enlist. Perhaps my ignorance on this matter wasn't really that surprising because I knew very little about my family background, only that my parents had moved down from Yorkshire shortly before I was born.

All in all, the war didn't have a great impact on me either. Of course, it was headline news when Germany bombed Harrow in 1940, but other than air raid drills at school, when we all had to run to the playground shed and put on our gas masks, not a lot changed. I also learned later that we'd been subjected to food rationing, but since my diet mainly consisted of porridge, dripping sandwiches, mashed potatoes, and cabbage with either a sausage or a leg of rabbit, I never really noticed the difference.

I was around nine years of age when a simple act had a profound and lasting effect on me. Following a playdate at Grace's house, her mother said, "Thanks for coming over, Shirley. We really enjoy your company, and you know you're always welcome here." Then she gave me a big hug and kissed my cheek. It was then when it finally registered with me that my mother had never shown me either appreciation or affection of any kind! I believe this event also triggered an increasing awareness of the relationship between my parents, as well as mine with them.

My father worked in the men's clothing section of a department store, and my mother often reminded me and anyone else who happened to be listening that he was the deputy manager. Years later, I discovered that, in fact, he was only another assistant, but because of his years of service, he had taken responsibility for his section when the manager was off sick or on vacation.

Each morning, my father would set off to work wearing a three-piece suit, a stiff white collar, and a bow tie. Around five o'clock, my mother would start to listen anxiously until she heard his key entering the door latch, at which time she would drop whatever she was doing and run to the scullery to make tea. I think she felt it would be a catastrophic failure on her part if she didn't deliver a cup to her husband's side within moments of him entering the sitting room. When my father arrived, his idea of relaxing would entail unbuttoning his shirt collar, loosening his tie, and handing his jacket to my mother. Having done that, he'd sit down and read the newspaper. Thirty minutes later, dinner would be served, and we'd generally eat in silence.

After dinner, my father would return to his armchair while my mother and I cleared the table and washed the dishes. When we returned to the sitting room, my mother would fuss around my father but rarely say anything of consequence. During this time, he would continue to read his paper or occasionally listen to the wireless. On odd occasions, he would ask about my day; though invariably, he returned to his newspaper before I'd finished answering.

*   *   *   *

Grace had always been taller than me, but when we hit our teenage years, other physical differences unfolded. Her body took on a new curvy shape while mine remained largely unchanged. Outside the classroom, Grace spent much of her time engaged in sports and country dancing, and a growing number of her friends were members of the opposite sex. I, on the other hand, spent most of my free time alone in the bedroom, either reading or painting. Remarkably, and for reasons that I really couldn't explain, our friendship remained firmly intact.

*   *   *   *

I'd just turned fourteen when the war ended, and I was looking forward to the following summer as I'd be leaving school, optimistic this would mark the beginning of a new and hopefully more exciting existence.

Christmas came and went, which was easy to miss in our home as my parents were atheists and thought Yuletide celebrations to be a waste of time and money. Eventually, July arrived and three weeks later so did my final day at school. I'd intended to start looking for a job during the summer holidays, but that plan changed when out of the blue, my father informed me that I'd be working for a local dressmaker, beginning the following Monday!

Though it wasn't a job that appealed to me, I didn't have the fortitude to defy my father. Instead, I decided to adopt a positive attitude and embrace the opportunity. When I arrived for my first day, I was told that in due course, I'd be taught how to cut cloth and sew. My initial duties, however, consisted only of sweeping floors, picking up and sorting off-cuts, and making tea for the supervisor. I tried to remain patient, but six months later, nothing had changed

I shared my plight with Grace one weekend. "You have to take charge of your life," she told me. "If you're unhappy with your current job then find another one."

In Grace's world, everything appeared to be straightforward. If a problem existed, you simply grabbed it by the scruff of the neck and solved it. I badly wanted to be like her, but I found myself incapable of addressing an increasingly frustrating situation.

Now that I was in the working world; my attraction towards boys increased, but unlike Grace, I was unable to find one who showed any interest in me. Initially, I put it down to their immaturity, but gradually, I arrived at an inevitable and demoralizing conclusion. Grace was pretty, and I wasn't. I spent hours looking at myself in the bathroom mirror, though even when I changed my posture or applied a little makeup, the image barely changed. Whereas Grace had the classic hourglass figure, the most flattering description I could give to mine was slim. Slim may have been an understatement; for although I now wore a bra, it wasn't necessary for support!

When 1947 arrived, I was thoroughly depressed. I still got together with Grace on occasion, but a busy social life took up much of her spare time. We mainly met on Saturday mornings when we'd either go window shopping or take a walk through the park. At lunch time, we visited the fish shop, where we'd share a three-penny bag of chips soaked in vinegar and covered with a healthy sprinkling of salt. Grace would tell me all about the boys she'd met and the fun she was having working at the hairdressing salon. I, on the other hand, had little to say about my life, and though I was happy for Grace, I suppose, at the same time, I may have been a little jealous.

That summer, I had my sixteenth birthday. My parents did buy me a pair of earrings, but that was the extent of the celebration I shared with them. The following Saturday, Grace took me to the morning matinee performance at the local cinema and then on to the pie and mash shop as a birthday treat. During the meal, Grace said, "I've got a surprise present that I'm going to give you later. One that I'm certain you're going to enjoy!"

"You've already been more than generous, Grace. I hope you didn't spend too much on spoiling me."

"Why have friends if you can't spoil them? Anyway, what I have for you didn't cost me a single penny," Grace said with a cheeky smile.

Aware that Grace wasn't someone who could be readily persuaded, I didn't dig for further information, knowing she'd tell me more when she was good and ready. Though I must say, my curiosity was aroused.

Following our lunch, we walked down to the cafe for a cup of tea. Knowing that Grace had an engagement at 3 o'clock, I was in the process of thanking Grace for the day out and taking my leave when she said, "Sit down for a moment, Shirley. I've still got to give you the surprise present that I mentioned earlier." I'd known she'd been seeing a boy named Billy for several weeks, but I hadn't heard mention of his friend, Paul. Grace gave me a smile that would light up any room before saying, "Paul is interested in meeting you, so I've arranged for the four of us to go out next

Saturday!" My self-confidence had got to the point where the very thought of spending time with a boy made me nervous. In spite of this, I knew Grace was only thinking about my happiness, and I was grateful.

Later in the week, Grace told me that we'd be meeting the boys at the local common on Saturday afternoon, as this would provide an opportunity for me to get to know Paul before we spent the evening at the local youth club.

After lunch on Saturday, I took a bath before contemplating what to wear. It wasn't as if I had numerous choices, but I tried on every conceivable combination of my limited wardrobe, finally settling on a floral pattern skirt and a white blouse. Then I went to the bathroom so I could see myself in the mirror. Despite willing my chest to expand, the reflection wouldn't cooperate. In an act of desperation, I ran back to my room and shoved two handkerchiefs inside each bra cup before returning to see what the mirror said. I was satisfied with the improvement and prayed that I wouldn't suffer the embarrassment of the handkerchiefs coming dislodged during the evening's activities.

I'd been wondering all week what Paul looked like, several times fearing the worst. But when I finally set eyes on him, I was pleasantly surprised. Handsome wouldn't be the first word that came to mind, though he was tall and nicely dressed. He seemed quite friendly, though we did have a difficult time finding topics of mutual interest. Fortunately, Grace was on hand to keep everything flowing, and, all in all, it ended up being an enjoyable evening.

Following our Saturday night out, Grace called for me unexpectedly on Wednesday. She said Paul had told Billy that he liked me, and she'd arranged for the four of us to meet up again. I suppose I was pleased, though I would have preferred if Paul had asked me in person!

Following the second double date, we quickly became a regular quartet, rarely socializing with anyone else. By and large, I was content with the arrangement, as time spent in Grace's company made me happy, and her presence avoided the necessity of relying only on my relationship with Paul, which frankly, never really sparkled.

*   *   *   *

Almost eighteen months had passed since the four of us first met up when one evening, Grace called to ask if we could meet alone on the coming Saturday, as she had something important to tell me. My first thought was that her relationship with Billy had gone awry, but when I asked about this, she kept quiet, saying she'd tell me her news the next weekend.

It occurred to me that if Grace and Billy had broken up, it was unlikely I'd continue seeing Paul. I soon realized this prospect didn't overly concern me, though at the time, I failed to comprehend the full implications of that thought.

When Grace arrived on Saturday, I tried to gauge her mood, sure she'd be upset if she'd parted ways with Billy. But during our walk to the local park, she was her usual lively self. While I tried to remain patient, I found my anxiety growing when after more than thirty minutes she still hadn't given me her news. Unsure if this was just Grace's normal personality at work or if for some unknown reason she was stringing me along, I reluctantly refrained from asking the question at the forefront of my mind. In true fashion, Grace had just finished relaying a funny story about an incident at the hairdressing salon, when she suddenly said loudly, "I have something of real importance to tell you, Shirley!"

At first, I wondered if she was trying to make light of a serious situation, until I heard the full story.

To say that I was speechless would have been a gross under-statement, but assuming I'd be thrilled, Grace gave me a huge hug before kissing my cheek and congratulating me. It seemed like an age before I was able to respond, and when I tried to, I was almost incoherent. On reflection, I doubt many young women with my disposition would have acted differently. After all, who would expect to be told that a double wedding had been proposed and that your best friend is hoping you will agree to be one of the brides!

I still find it hard to believe, but after getting over the initial shock, I went along with the idea, most likely because I didn't want to rock the boat, or perhaps, I feared the outcome of having no other attractive option. During the following weeks, when the arrangements were being planned, I felt sure I must be dreaming, but of course, if I was, I didn't wake up!

Finally, the big day arrived, and I spent the morning at Grace's house getting myself ready. She helped with my hair and makeup, and we wore matching dresses that I'd had tailored in the shop where I worked. When it came time for me to say, "I do," I answered as if the question wasn't really aimed at me but rather as if I were a remote character watching an image of myself from high above.

The reception was held in the youth club gymnasium, with a small area set aside to be used as a dance floor. As it turned out, I ended up spending more time dancing with Grace than my new husband, who, together with his dad, rarely left the bar. And as one would suspect, both of them were very drunk by the time the event finished. Actually, it didn't bother me much at the time, as I assumed this was just a normal father and son tradition. On reflection, I suppose I should have taken more notice. One thing that did surprise me, however, was my parents' jocular mood. Call me cynical, but I later came to conclude their joy was largely a result of my moving out of the family home rather than me becoming Mrs. Shirley Weller!

We spent our first night together in Paul's parents' spare room. Needless to say, there was no romance or intimacy, as Paul immediately fell to sleep while still fully dressed.

The next morning we got up early in order to catch a train to Manchester then a coach ride that would take the four of us to North Wales. Paul hardly said a word on the journey, presumably because he was still nursing a severe hangover, but as usual, Grace kept us all entertained.

The bed and breakfast establishment where we were to spend ten days was in a beautiful location, surrounded by tree-lined hills and close to a lake. By evening time, Paul had returned to something more resembling his normal self, assisted, I suspect, by the consumption of more beer; though when we turned in for the night, he didn't appear to be drunk.

Naturally, I was full of anticipation at the prospect of finally losing my virginity, but regrettably, the experience wasn't what I'd hoped it would be. I discussed this alone with Grace the following day, who assured me things would improve over time. Clearly, this subject wasn't an issue with her, and for the first time, I wondered if she had still been a virgin the previous evening. I got my answer four weeks later when she told me that she was three months pregnant.

Apart from disappointment in the bedroom, overall, the honeymoon turned out to be quite enjoyable. The accommodations were delightful, the food delicious, and we spent many hours walking around the glorious countryside together. We also took boat rides on the nearby lake. By the time we returned to Paul's parents' house, our first home as a married couple, I felt a little more optimistic about my future.

CHAPTER 6

Initially, living in the spare room at Paul's parents' home provided a welcome change of scenery, but within a matter of weeks, I found myself slowly returning to another humdrum existence. Furthermore, in the process of spending time alone with Paul, I quickly discovered that we had even less in common than I'd previously feared, and our conversations soon became limited, to say the very least. I suppose I should have foreseen this, as subconsciously, I knew Grace had always been the glue that kept us together, but regrettably, that time had now passed.

Being in Paul's company became increasingly awkward, often with long deafening periods of silence, and it wasn't long before he started spending most evenings down at the pub with his dad. At first, I'd talk with his mother when they were gone, but I soon discovered that I had little in common with her either! Consequently, a routine was established; I'd help with the preparation of dinner and the clearing up afterwards, but then found myself primarily spending time alone in our room, either reading or painting to keep occupied.

Now that we were both wed, Grace and I saw less of each other, though we typically met up briefly on Sundays. Clearly, marriage was suiting her, and our conversations became dominated by matters of motherhood as her due date grew closer. This was a subject that I no longer expected to be associated with, as Paul clearly had no interest in starting a family and, with our evolving relationship, neither did I. That's not to imply that he completely lacked the normal urges of a young man, but rather, he seemed incapable of showing love or engaging in an act of true intimacy. By the time we'd been married for six months, I gave up hoping this would change, and frankly was pleased that on the odd occasion Paul climbed clumsily on top of me, it was only a matter of moments before he rolled off and went to sleep.

In early November 1949, Grace gave birth to a six-pound baby boy, who they named William. Grace had always been outgoing and optimistic, and the birth of her son only enhanced these qualities.

The Christmas season arrived, and after helping with paper chain decorations and cooking the turkey, I was at least looking forward to a few relaxing days away from work. Paul's mother and I planned to serve a traditional lunch at 1 pm on Christmas Day, thereby allowing Paul and his dad to pop down to the local pub for a pint or two beforehand. When they returned at 2:30 pm, it didn't take a genius to diagnose their condition. Paul went straight to the bathroom where he threw up, and his dad slumped in the armchair seconds before passing out.

By the time I returned to work in the New Year, I was at an all-time low. To make matters worse, I now felt trapped. Divorce was heavily frowned upon in my social circles, and the only female I knew in such a predicament was spoken down to and largely avoided by all and sundry. In any event, where could I go, and what would I do if I left Paul? My spirits continued to decline until something totally unexpected took place. My periods had often been out of cycle, so I hadn't taken much notice for a couple of weeks, but I thought a visit with the doctor may be in order. I was dumbfounded when he told me I was pregnant.

Carrying my child gave me a new sense of purpose. Ironically, it gave Paul an opportunity to brag about his sexual prowess. In my new condition, the boredom of work life and my disappointment with marriage seemed to fade, as I now had a new focus. Grace shared my excitement, and naturally, our conversations turned largely to child-rearing.

Nine months passed quickly, and after a short and uncomplicated period of labor, I gave birth to a five-pound baby girl. While Paul normally liked to dominate family decisions, naming our daughter was something I felt very strongly about. Consequently, I was relieved when he agreed, albeit reluctantly, to my choice of 'Sophie'.

Being a mother raised my self-confidence as well as my morale, but it did little or nothing to improve matters between Paul and me. Though he often showed off his daughter to friends and family, he didn't spend time with her, and I sensed an underlying resentment towards us both.

Now with a child, we were able to apply for council accommodations, and shortly after celebrating Sophie's first birthday, we moved into a two-bedroom terraced council house. With our newfound privacy, I hoped and prayed Paul's attitude would improve, for although I'd long given up on his relationship with me, I desperately wanted our daughter to grow up in a loving environment or, at the very least, an appearance of one. But Paul didn't respond the way I'd hoped. Instead, he started to complain about the extra costs and make derogatory comments regarding my lack of contribution to our income. Of course, he had no practical suggestions when I asked what he expected me to do; he simply became more angry and obnoxious.

By the time Sophie was two years of age, contact with my husband was limited to putting meals in front of him when he came home, taking care of his laundry, and answering his pointed and sarcastic questions, normally about housekeeping expenses. Typically, he'd disappear down to the pub after eating dinner, and most evenings, Sophie and I were asleep in bed before he arrived back home.

While I continued to be frustrated by the impractical dissolution of my marriage, having Sophie provided a source of joy for me. Fortunately, she had a sunny disposition, and now that she was talking, our time together allowed me to forget about the other aspects of my life, at least most of the time. Additionally, Sophie shared my love of drawing, and we'd spend countless hours working on projects together. Every bedtime was also special, as she'd snuggle up to my side while I read stories until she was overcome by sleep, which gave her the look of an angel.

I found myself wishing life for Sophie and I would continue the way it had always been, half hoping she'd never grow up. But of course, her first day of school eventually arrived. Paul was as difficult and stingy as ever, and I had to do without in order to buy Sophie two school uniforms. I didn't doubt she would do well in class, as she could already read and write quite proficiently, but my concern was her anxiety at being away from me for the first time.

As I waved goodbye when we reached the entrance door of the infant school, I held my breath and ran around the corner before bursting into tears. Back outside the entrance door six hours later, I stood nervously, hoping Sophie had been able to handle the shock of separation. I would later find out from other mothers that it's not unusual for the parent to have more difficulty dealing with this experience than the child does. This was certainly the case with me, as I'd spent all day worrying myself sick, while my daughter had thoroughly enjoyed meeting her teacher and the other students, barely giving me a second thought!

CHAPTER 7

For the first few weeks after Sophie started school, I felt a void in my life. After dropping her off each morning, I'd be back home by nine o'clock, and even after completing daily chores and shopping when necessary, I normally had two or three hours on my hands before collecting her.

I decided to fill in my days by painting landscapes again, rather than the small projects I'd done with Sophie for the last couple of years. I didn't have much spare money, but over a period of weeks, I managed to put enough aside to purchase some basic art materials. Knowing Paul would complain if he thought I'd wasted money on what he saw as a pointless hobby, I told him they were a gift from an old school friend.

One morning, Paul asked me to buy him some rolling tobacco, as the store close to the factory where he always bought his supplies had closed for a week due to repairs. I was waiting in line at the tobacconist's when I happened to glance at the notice board that was hanging next to the counter. There was a sign saying, *Part-time filing clerk wanted*, written in small black letters.

After completing my purchase, I went back to the notice board to read the details. It didn't provide much information other than saying hours could be flexible and the phone number for interested applicants to call.

Employment hadn't crossed my mind since Sophie's arrival, as it seemed impractical. However, I'd never given part-time work any thought and found myself staring at the sign, wondering if perhaps it was an option. I decided it probably wouldn't work for me, but as I was leaving the shop, I went back and scribbled down the phone number in my diary in the unlikely event that I changed my mind.

Given I was busy the following day, I'd forgotten about the advertisement until the time to collect Sophie was approaching. On the spur of the moment, I rushed to the phone booth at the end of our road and dialed the number written in my diary. When the gentleman at the other end answered, I was tempted to hang up thinking it unlikely they'd want to hire me anyway. But before I was able to respond, he asked if I was calling about the opening, and he said he could meet me for an interview at 10:30 the following morning.

Unlike most evenings when I fell asleep exhausted but content from the day's activities, I found myself restless, thinking about the following day. The next morning after taking Sophie to school, I had second thoughts about the job prospect. Having pretty much decided not to show up, I suddenly changed my mind again, rationalizing that I really had nothing to lose. I dashed home, took a quick bath, and put on a dress I thought suitable for office attire and a pair of sensible shoes. The gentleman had given me directions to his office, and being familiar with the area, I judged it to be a twenty-minute walk.

Fortunately, I found the place without a problem and checked in with the receptionist at 10:20. There, I was shown to a small waiting room, and five minutes later, the gentleman I'd spoken with arrived and asked me to follow him to his office.

I'm sure he must have noticed my nervousness, as I could feel my voice quivering when I answered each of his questions. On the way home, I tried to recall what had just taken place. I had trouble recollecting all the details, but I did remember him asking me to phone in two days, as he'd have made a decision by then.

Later that day, I began to think it would hardly be hardly worth the four pennies it cost for a phone call, so I tried to put the whole issue out of my mind, concluding it had been nothing short of a fool's errand. But two days later, I found myself back in the phone booth, concentrating on dialing the correct number.

As one ring followed another, I felt certain my call wasn't going to be answered. I wondered if perhaps they'd guessed it was me calling, and they'd already given the job to someone else. With my self-confidence rapidly spiraling downwards, I tried to console myself. It had only occurred to me that hanging up and pushing button 'B' would at least return my money when suddenly a voice came on the line. You could have knocked me down with a feather when I heard the words, "Yes, Mrs. Weller, you have the job, and we look forward to seeing you on Monday morning."

That evening over dinner, I told Paul my news. He didn't seem to care one way or the other, though he did say that it was about time I earned my keep, followed by him pointedly telling me he could now reduce my housekeeping allowance accordingly! I'd rarely spoken any untruths in my life, and the few I had could be safely categorized as white lies. Even telling these normally made me feel terrible, but I felt no sense of guilt whatsoever when I told Paul my wages were five shillings less than what I'd actually been offered!

Excited by the prospect of something new in my life, Grace and I spent Saturday afternoon taking our children to the local common for a picnic. When Sunday arrived, I took time out to wash and set my hair before ironing the dress I'd selected to wear for my first day at work. Anticipating a new adventure, I climbed into bed early, took a deep breath, and tried hard to relax, though I was unable to prevent my mind jumping from subject to subject. I tried counting sheep, and in desperation, I started to read, which, fortunately, slowly allowed my body to drift into sleep.

On Monday morning, I dropped Sophie off at school a few minutes earlier than usual then dashed back to the house to get myself ready. Knowing precisely how long the walk took, I gave myself a ten-minute cushion, just in case. The office was located in the High Street above a grocery store, and access to it was up a narrow staircase. Mrs. Hodges, the firm's receptionist and typist, met me when I arrived and accompanied me into the meeting room where a fresh pot of tea was waiting.

I'd seen Mrs. Hodges on my previous visit and had judged her to be aloof and perhaps a little arrogant. But I was quick to find out that hidden behind those steel-rimmed glasses and stern face was a warm and kind lady. She proceeded to tell me about herself, together with details of the firm and my responsibilities. Mrs. Hodges was a widow in her early sixties, having lost her husband during the Great War. The firm was owned by Mr. Fitzpatrick, a professional accountant who provided services to small local businesses. Mrs. Hodges' husband had been a schoolboy friend of Mr. Fitzpatrick, and she had been with the firm for thirty years. There were two other members of staff, both book-keepers. The previous filing clerk had left earlier in the month when her husband relocated to a new job in Bristol. My role would be organizing copies of the daily letters that were sent out, together with incoming mail, and filing all of them in chronological and subject order. She showed me how to find existing files and how to set up new ones. Luckily, it only took an hour or so before I felt comfortable with what was expected of me.

Mrs. Hodges went on to tell me that she would always be available if I had questions. She told me never to hesitate to ask questions even for matters that I might think trivial, as it was imperative mistakes be avoided at all costs. Coming from another individual, I may have found this last directive to be condescending, but somehow, Mrs. Hodges made it sound like a collaborative effort.

I'd already been told that the weekly compensation was twenty-five shillings for twenty hours, but Mrs. Hodges went on to explain a flexible component of the arrangement that may be beneficial on occasion. Each day I should plan on working for four hours, starting no earlier than nine o'clock. If I wanted to take a break for lunch or to run errands, I simply had to sign out and complete the balance of outstanding time when I returned. In addition, if my daily tasks were completed in less than four hours, I could leave for the day without deduction in pay. Naturally, I was thrilled to hear this arrangement, as it provided the opportunity to have flexibility with my daughter's schedule and other household obligations if needed. Mrs. Hodges didn't say anything at the time, but I was to find out later that she'd devised the plan, having convinced Mr. Fitzpatrick he'd get more loyalty from a filing clerk if he made allowances for their personal life.

From the very first day, I was happy with my new job. It wasn't overly taxing or exciting, but I had to keep my wits about me to avoid mistakes, something I now felt was a matter of honor. The other staff members were always busy, so although there was little social interaction, they were always polite and friendly, and consequently, the office was a place where I felt both welcome and secure.

CHAPTER 

In early 1956, Grace gave birth to a six-pound baby girl who she named Shirley. This act amounted to the greatest gesture of friendship and appreciation she could have possibly bestowed on yours truly—and something I would always hold near and dear to my heart. She'd been trying to get pregnant again for more than a year, and with Shirley's arrival, her and Billy's family dreams were complete.

I continued visiting Grace whenever possible, but because of her increased commitments, we didn't spend as much time together as in days past; nevertheless, the closeness we'd formed over the years remained intact. When we did meet up, Grace spoke lovingly about her family, and despite the challenges of providing for two children on a very tight budget, she always seemed in a state of bliss.

I'm not sure if Grace had much insight into my true relationship with Paul, as I generally avoided the subject or sugar-coated it if needs be. Frankly, I'm not sure why I did this, as I'd always been able to talk openly with her in the past on any matter. Perhaps it was because I didn't want her to feel guilty, given her role in how my marriage came about, or maybe, it was easier to ignore reality and act as if all was well. Of course, Paul and Billy remained friends, occasionally going to the pub together for a pint and, during the winter, watching Arsenal's home games. Though I'm not absolutely certain, I'm pretty sure Paul pretended his marriage was happy and stable when talking with friends and family, and though it would be hard to believe, maybe he really thought it was!

Talking of family, after my wedding, I saw very little of my parents. They never visited me, and I only popped round to their house once a fortnight, as I felt an obligation to do so. When I did, however, I invariably got a sense that it was inconvenient for them, and typically, after a brief and normally awkward conversation, I'd make up some excuse as to why I had to leave early. To top matters off, this situation didn't change even after Sophie's birth. When I arrived to show her off for the first time, my mother stared from a distance, giving the impression that she didn't want any physical contact with my daughter, and though my father managed to force a smile, he hardly said a word either! I suppose I wasn't really surprised, though I have to admit I was still bitterly disappointed. Despite their first reaction, I continued to live in the hope that they'd warm up to their granddaughter as she grew older, but this was not to be. While they always sent her a birthday card, the greeting never included so much as a kiss, a hug, or any other sign of affection, just the words "From your grandparents."

*   *   *   *

In October 1956, Sophie turned six years of age. To celebrate, I promised to take her to see the Saturday morning children's program at the local cinema, followed by a visit to the corner shop that sold ice cream. I was shocked when Paul said he wanted to join us and wondered if this might represent a step in a new direction for him. It didn't take long, however, to realize the gesture was only intended to impress his parents, as he sat through both films either fidgeting or closing his eyes for extended periods of time. To add fuel to the fire, later in the day, he repeatedly mentioned the sacrifice he'd made to join us, which meant missing a key Gunners league match!

Despite Paul's selfish and uncaring behavior, Sophie and I had a good time, and as the weekend weather stayed fine, we spent most of Sunday at the park.

Back at work on Monday morning, I took a brief lunch break and found myself reflecting on life as I strolled down the High Street window shopping. I concluded that "I'd made my bed," and as the saying goes, "I had to lie in it." However, I took some satisfaction from having a beautiful, loving daughter and a job where at least I was appreciated.

The following weekend, I visited Grace to find her busily knitting a sweater for William. Then she showed me some of the clothes she'd made for Billy, including a red and white pullover with *I love Arsenal* and *Go Gunners* embroidered on the back. With winter approaching, I knew Sophie could do with a wooly hat and scarf, something I mentioned to Grace. "I don't understand why you don't make them yourself. It's much cheaper than buying readymade knitwear," she said, in her usual inimitable way. When I told Grace I couldn't knit, she laughed and, in predictable style, said she could teach me in no time at all. Though I was skeptical, I decided to take her up on the offer, and to my delight, I soon became quite proficient. I promised Grace that I'd work on this new project as soon as possible, so when I felt ready, she told me about a shop that sold wool and knitting accessories at discounted prices. It turned out to be located only a couple of blocks from my office, so I made a mental note to visit the following day if circumstances allowed.

The following morning, I asked Sophie her preference of color, and when lunch time came around, I signed out, telling Mrs. Hodges I had an errand to run, so I'd be gone for at least forty-five minutes. The wool shop was only a five-minute walk, although I'd never been down that particular road before. When I arrived, I found some purple yarn that I knew Sophie would love, so I purchased a sufficient amount for a matching hat and scarf.

Not being in a rush, I decided to take a different route back to the office so I could check out the shops. I'd almost reached the High Street when I noticed a café with a sign in the window that caught my attention. It read *Large bowl of homemade tomato soup together with bread and butter—sixpence.* Tomato soup had always been a favorite of mine, and something told me a homemade version would be extra special. Given that I now had five shillings a week my husband was unaware of, I promised to treat myself one day rather than eat the sandwich I normally took for lunch. I had planned to go later in the week, but due to the heavy rain, I delayed my trip until the following Tuesday. Determined to make the most of it, I told Mrs. Hodges I'd be taking a full hour lunch break, so at noon I set off, taking with me the book I was currently reading.

"Large bowl of homemade tomato soup, please," I told the grey-haired elderly lady serving behind the counter, who, after taking my money, told me I could sit wherever I wanted, and my meal would be delivered to me shortly. There weren't many people in the café, but I chose to sit in the far corner thinking it would give me more privacy. Three or four minutes later, my soup arrived accompanied by two large slices of brown bread, each amply covered in butter.

I took a sip, and to my delight, it was even better than I'd imagined it might be. I opened my book at the page where I'd left off the previous evening and started reading. I'd already figured out that if I drank one spoonful of soup after finishing each page, I could make my treat last until it was time to head back to work even if it had gone cold by then!

The last spoonful came more quickly than I'd hoped, so I marked my page and slipped the book into my handbag. For the first time since sitting down, I looked up, and three tables diagonally opposite of mine, there was an attractive gentleman reading while at the same time consuming a bowl of soup. I don't know if the sound of my chair scraping on the floor caught his attention, but at that very instant, he looked up, and our eyes met. He had dark curly hair and freckles, and when he smiled, I felt a warm sensation flow through my body, which made me momentarily stop in my tracks.

Suddenly conscious that I was staring at a stranger, I felt myself blush. Quickly, I tried to regain my composure and, upon doing so, proceeded towards the exit to avoid further embarrassment. But as I passed his table, he asked through a sweet smile, "Are you enjoying *Black Beauty*?" More than a little flustered, I muttered awkwardly, "Yes, I am." In truth, I would have liked to talk further, as something about the man attracted me. But in typical fashion, I found myself unwittingly saying that I was in a hurry before scampering out the door.

Back at the office, I returned to my duties; though for reasons I didn't fully comprehend, I had trouble focusing on my work.

CHAPTER 9

The morning after treating myself at the café, I awoke with a clear image in my head of the man I'd seen the previous day. I didn't give it too much thought at the time; though subsequently, it became difficult to ignore, as during the following days, the same image reappeared on a regular basis. I tried to rationalize why this was happening, but even after considerable thought, nothing made sense. Yes, of course there was something about him that attracted me, though I'd seen better-looking men who I'd forgotten about within minutes. And it wasn't as if we'd had a meaningful conversation, for our interaction had only lasted a matter of seconds.

After driving myself half mad thinking about what was, after all, an irrelevant incident, I made a conscious effort to focus on other subjects. But try as I may, I still couldn't get the man out of my mind. Attempting to use logic rather than emotion, I concluded the only sensible thing to do was make a return trip to the café and see if he still held an attraction for me. If so, perhaps I could strike up a conversation; if not, I reasoned it would be easy to forget about him once and for all.

In preparation for my planned reunion, I finished reading *Black Beauty*, rationalizing that it might provide a suitable platform from which to start a meaningful conversation—if events ever led in that direction!

At lunch time on Tuesday, I signed out of the office and, full of anticipation, set off to the café, where I ordered soup before taking the same spot that I'd occupied the previous week. I took another book with me and began reading it while slowly drinking my soup. As the minutes passed, it dawned on me that the gentleman may not be a regular, and likely, his last visit was just a one-off occasion. I could have kicked myself when I saw how stupid I'd been in getting my hopes up, and the minute I finished my soup, I got up and stomped off feeling like a complete fool.

Later that evening, when Sophie had gone to sleep, I reflected on my day and came to a depressing conclusion. Clearly, my life lacked a loving and fulfilling partner, and I'd managed to convince myself that I'd met a nice man who may become a good friend and, as a result, help fill that void in my life. To make matters even worse, it occurred to me that my hopes had arisen based on ridiculous assumptions; for even if I had bumped into him again, why on earth would he have any interest in me? Concluding that the whole episode was nothing more than an inevitable consequence of my pathetic existence, I took some comfort in being certain that I could now put the subject out of my mind once and for all.

*   *   *   *

Following my café episodes, I turned my attention back to painting. I'd recently completed a couple of landscapes using photographs of the Swiss Alps as inspiration, and to my delight, this activity stirred Sophie's interest. Wanting to develop this further if possible, I suggested we go to the park on Saturday, in order that she could sketch trees and flowers and color them in afterwards.

Our outing turned out to be a great success, and the look in Sophie's eyes conveyed the joy so many people experience from producing art. Apart from seeing in her a reflection of myself at a younger age, it also made me feel very proud.

Starting with a simple beginning, Sophie now wanted to spend most weekends sketching and painting, so I took her to several nearby locations that provided a variety of scenes for her to copy. To keep her motivation going, I promised Sophie that if her skills improved and she maintained the same level of interest, I'd buy her a proper drawing book together with a large paint box as an early birthday present. In the meantime, one of the book-keepers at the office, who also liked to paint, recommended an art supply outlet store that was only a short distance away.

The following Wednesday, the filing load was lighter than usual, so at 11:30 am, I checked out, knowing the balance of my day's work could easily be completed after an hour's break. I found the store without difficulty and proceeded to browse around the items on display. My co-worker proved to be dead-on, as both the brushes and oils were less expensive than I'd paid previously, plus they offered a far greater variety of supplies. I also saw a small easel that I thought Sophie would like, and though I was tempted to purchase it, I decided I'd bring her with me at the weekend in order to make sure it was one that she liked. When the large clock hanging above the cashiers counter indicated it was just past noon, I paid for my purchases and set off back to the office. Without a need to hurry, I decided to take the route that passed the café; I was curious to see if they had any other specials on offer. I'd just passed the sign that still read *Homemade tomato soup* when a voice from behind me said, "So, did you enjoy *Black Beauty*?" I didn't need to guess who'd spoken the words, and when I turned around, his smile and manner had the same effect on me as the last time we'd last met!

I tried to collect myself and told the gentleman that I'd be happy to discuss the story another day, but now, I needed to rush. As soon as the words left my mouth, I knew they'd not portrayed the message or tone I'd intended and was certain he'd think of me as abrupt and curt. Embarrassed and upset with myself, I took off quickly, but I'd only gone a few steps when he appeared alongside me and asked if I could join him the following day at the café. I tried hard not to look overly excited at this unlikely turn of events and accepted his offer as calmly as I could.

That evening after Sophie went to bed, I made tea for myself and sat down to contemplate tomorrow's lunch date. I could hardly contain myself and at the same time, I wasn't exactly sure why I was experiencing such feelings. I kept wondering, *What do I hope will come from this?* In truth, I didn't really know. Eventually, I persuaded myself to have no lofty expectations, as the last thing I wanted was to experience even further disappointment in my life!

The next morning I walked Sophie to school and then hurried home. There, I put on my best dress and my highest heels before applying a little face powder and lipstick. Upon entering the office, it occurred to me that I'd never dressed this way before, and I wondered if it would draw anyone's attention. Fortunately, there was no mention of my appearance, though I think Mrs. Hodges smiled at me for a little longer than usual!

Two hours passed slowly, but eventually, the clock struck twelve. On my walk to the café, I could feel my heart beating faster, so I tried to compensate by taking deep breathes. In spite of efforts to calm down, I still found myself struggling to talk normally when I ordered my soup, which caused the server to give me a sideways look and ask if everything was all right. After giving her suitable assurance, I took the same seat in the far corner and started reading my book until the soup arrived.

As the minutes ticked by, I found myself trying to remember the brief conversation from the previous day. I'd had it in mind that we were meeting at 12:15, but as it was now 12:20, I wondered if in the excitement of the moment I'd misunderstood the arrangement, or worse still, he wasn't going to show up!

By 12:25, I was vacillating between disappointment and mild anger when suddenly the gentleman appeared through the doorway. He smiled and waved at me before proceeding to the counter and placing his order.

"Sorry I'm a bit late. Got delayed in a meeting with my supervisor," he said apologetically when he arrived at the table where I was sitting. I couldn't have been more nervous, but in short order, we were busy chatting about *Black Beauty* and other works that we'd both read. We'd moved on to the subject of art when, to my horror, I noticed it was 1:15. Interpreting my reaction when I looked at my wristwatch, he said, "I'm guessing you need to get somewhere else quickly," to which I offered what I immediately felt was a weak apology. It wasn't the way I wanted the meeting to end, but to my relief, he asked if I'd like to continue our conversation the following Tuesday. I told him that I would like to, and as I got up to leave, he added, "Goodness, please excuse my bad manners, but I forgot to introduce myself. My name's Ralph."

"And mine's Shirley," I replied before running out the door.

Mrs. Hodges gave me a sideways look when I arrived twenty-five minutes later than expected. Knowing it may break the trust we'd built up if I didn't say something, I apologized and explained that I'd unexpectedly bumped into an old friend and lost track of time. I think she may have had an inclination, but she smiled and said it wasn't an issue. She simply reminded me to make sure my work was finished before I left for the day.

As always, I had an enjoyable weekend with Sophie though I often found myself preoccupied, willing Tuesday to arrive. I'd only spent one hour with Ralph and wondered why sixty short minutes had such an impact on me when suddenly it dawned on me. For many years, conversations with my husband, albeit increasingly limited and infrequent, were typically initiated by necessity or anger. Whereas Ralph talked about subjects I enjoyed; additionally, he listened to my opinions with great interest. This made me feel very special, especially since he was the first male in my life ever to do so!

Tuesday eventually arrived, and as planned, we met at noon in order to give us the maximum possible time together. Sixty minutes flew by, and when it came time to leave, there was still so much I wanted to say. Our conversation focused on literature but also touched on history, a subject I discovered Ralph was well read on. Personal issues didn't crop up, and though I was keen to know more about his life, I believed it to be premature to lead the discussion in that direction. However, just before we parted, he said he'd like to get to know me better, and as he had travel plans for the following week, he suggested we meet again in a fortnight's time.

Our next get-together turned out to be the first of many regular weekly meetings, and with each one, I learned a little more about his background and circumstances. During this time, I also sensed a growing closeness between us. It took a couple of months before I felt comfortable asking a direct question about his marriage, and when I did, he went quiet for a while, which was totally out of character. Following a moment of silence, he reached across the table and took my hand, saying it was a subject he'd rather discuss in a more private setting. And before we both took off, he asked if we could meet in the local park on Saturday afternoon, as this would allow us to continue the conversation in a more private setting and without the same time constraints.

As luck would have it, Sophie had a school friend who occasionally invited her over to play, so I was able to arrange a date for them, giving myself the opportunity to spend a good part of the afternoon with Ralph.

The bus ride was only fifteen minutes, and after disembarking, I spotted him sitting on the bench as planned. While it wasn't a location that I frequented, I was still fearful of being seen alone with a man who was not my husband! To this end, I'd taken along a headscarf and a pair of sunglasses, hopeful these would act as a disguise if anyone who knew me happened to be passing by. Ralph laughed when he first saw me, though he subsequently agreed it was an appropriate precaution, and perhaps one he should take himself in the future. For the first time since we'd met, I saw a hint of sadness in his eyes as he began giving me an overview of his private life. He avoided going into detail; though reading between the lines, I detected many similarities with my own circumstances. I didn't want to harp on the subject, so I only told him a little about my relationship with Paul before changing gears and discussing the more interesting topics we both enjoyed.

It was nearly time for me to catch the bus home when Ralph said he wanted to show me something, and after taking my hand, we walked to a nearby crop of trees. Out of sight from other visitors, Ralph stopped and put his arms around me. He paid me several compliments while gazing lovingly into my eyes. With the warmth of his body permeating mine, I felt my physical desire rising. Finally, as if drawn together by magnets, our lips met. Naturally, I was fully aware that showing outward affection in public places was considered an inappropriate act for young women, but with the drop of a hat, any such feelings that I may have had instantly vanished! As the kiss continued, the intensity of our embrace increased, and when our mouths finally parted, I'd never felt so wanted and loved before. Torn between my desire to stay in Ralph's embrace and the likely consequences of being late to collect Sophie, I reluctantly said my goodbyes. But even when I went to bed that night, my body was still tingling with the wonderful sensation of our togetherness.

CHAPTER 10

Our clandestine get-togethers sparked a gradual increase in time spent together, as now we were normally able to have lunch once each week and meet up on those Saturdays when I was able to find someone to watch my daughter. Every minute with Ralph made me feel special and appreciated, but of course, I carried some measure of guilt, which was a natural consequence, I suppose, of my marital status.

I discovered that Ralph was born into a blue-collar family who lived just outside of Watford. When he left grammar school at age sixteen, he secured a job as a trainee maintenance engineer with a manufacturing company. One of the side benefits of the job, as Ralph jokingly pointed out to me, was that the business employed significantly more females than males!

The company was owned by Mr. and Mrs. Simpson, a wealthy couple who had a number of other business interests. The Simpsons had only one child, a daughter named Fiona, who'd been thoroughly spoiled since birth. Though Fiona suffered from facial acne and was considerably overweight, she acted as if she were the most desirable creature on planet Earth. Upon leaving school, Fiona's father made her a supervisor in the company. In operational terms, she had no real function or responsibilities, but rather, she enjoyed demonstrating her authority whenever it suited her cause. Almost all of the firm's female employees secretly disliked her but avoided showing their true feelings, being acutely aware that she could have them dismissed at a whim. Fiona often spent hours idly chatting with the female workforce with two objectives in mind—the first being to fill time, given she had little else to do, and the second, more importantly, was that it provided her an opportunity to boast about her success with men, believing this would reinforce the image she was keen to portray. While Fiona could undoubtedly offer a comfortable future to potential suitors, in fact, she'd had little success in this area despite her many claims to the contrary.

One day during a tea break, Fiona overheard a conversation between several young female workers, during which it was generally agreed upon that Ralph was an attractive and likeable young man, who'd be a good catch. On hearing this, Fiona's jealous nature got the better of her, especially as Ralph had never paid her any attention. Without forethought and driven solely by her ego, she told several workers that she was secretly dating Ralph. Later in the day however, she reflected on her outburst, and to her chagrin, she realized that the story she'd put out would almost certainly be found as untrue. Aware that the probable resulting embarrassment would be more than she could endure, she devised a plan aimed at avoiding such an outcome.

The next morning Fiona invited Ralph into her office under the pretext of having a work-related issue she wanted to discuss in private. On his arrival, she told him that she actually had a personal matter that she'd like his help with while inferring that his selection for the task should be taken as a privilege. She went on to explain that her parents owned a holiday cottage in the town of Rye on the south coast and that she'd been asked to spend a weekend there in order to get things ready for the upcoming summer season. While Fiona knew she couldn't force Ralph to accompany her, she dropped less than subtle hints that a refusal on his part would put his position with the firm in jeopardy. On the other hand, if he was agreeable, she would take steps to ensure a bright future for him.

Though Ralph profoundly resented the position he found himself in, he was keen to maintain his current employment, so after carefully considering the pros and cons, he reluctantly agreed to Fiona's request.

On getting Ralph's concurrence, Fiona took great pleasure in informing the girls at the factory that she was spending the weekend with Ralph at the seaside. Further, she rubbed it in by asking if they'd like her to bring them back a stick of Rye rock.

That Friday afternoon, Fiona collected Ralph in the family Land Rover, and together they headed down to the cottage, arriving in time for a late dinner. On Saturday morning, they took off for a walk along the beach, and following a light lunch, they shopped for provisions necessary to make the cottage visitor friendly. As the day wore on, Ralph begrudging found Fiona a little more agreeable than the picture of her that had been painted by other girls in the office, even though he suspected that she might just be putting on an act. But perhaps, he thought to himself, in the circumstances, he should give her the benefit of the doubt.

Later in the afternoon, Fiona left Ralph alone while she popped out to buy food for their dinner. On her return, she prepared fresh shellfish, together with a salad, and opened a bottle of expensive French white wine to compliment the meal. Ralph had never experienced a treat like this before and found crab sandwiches with raw oysters on the side something that he could quickly get used to. Fiona had done her homework, and as a result, she was able to keep Ralph's undivided attention as they chatted comfortably together over a glass of brandy.

When Fiona gauged Ralph's alcohol intake to be at an appropriate level, she told him that she'd heard about his talent for sketching. She'd gained this information from the maintenance division, who often provided handmade drawings of proposed changes to equipment. The maintenance workers told her that many of the drawings had been prepared by Ralph. She went on to ask Ralph if he'd sketch her likeness, and without waiting for a response, she took off to collect paper and pencils from the living room. In fact, Ralph was happy to do so, as he'd warmed up to Fiona, and additionally, the wine and brandy he'd consumed put him in a particularly agreeable mood. Despite his state of mild inebriation, he was nevertheless taken aback when Fiona proceeded to remove all her clothing before requesting that Ralph draw her lying down naked in a seductive pose.

Due to an unsteady hand and a slightly spinning head, Ralph's sketch did not do his talent justice, though Fiona told him the drawing was quite perfect. After complimenting Ralph on his work, she squatted on his lap and proceeded to teasingly rub her breasts slowly around his face. While Ralph had been on dates in the past, he'd never encountered such a provocative advance, and though he was a little embarrassed, he did nevertheless find his situation very arousing. His excitement reached a new level when Fiona unzipped his trousers and took him out; following which, she gently eased herself onto his manhood.

*   *   *   *

When Ralph first awoke on Sunday morning, he was unsure of his whereabouts. Suddenly, he realized that he was in bed with Fiona asleep beside him; the events of the previous evening gradually filled his mind. His head hurt from the amount of alcohol he'd drunk, but that wasn't what bothered him the most. Though some of the details were a little fuzzy, he knew he'd had sex with Fiona, and he searched his inner self trying desperately to understand why he'd allowed that to happen.

The journey home on Sunday was awkward for Ralph, as having fulfilled her mission and the bragging rights she sought, Fiona returned to her normal arrogant and boastful self. To make matters worse, she didn't try to conceal the fact that she would show Ralph's sketch to other workers if she chose to and warned him against contradicting anything she said about their weekend away.

Following Ralph's misadventure in Rye, Fiona proceeded to ignore him to demonstrate the control she held over him, and additionally, she wanted to prove her contentions to workers at the factory. On the one hand, Ralph was relieved at not having to deal further with Fiona; though on the other hand, he remained cognizant of her ability to bring his current employment to an abrupt end.

*　*　*　*

Six weeks had passed since Ralph's escapade in Rye; when one evening on his way home from work, he felt a tap on his shoulder. Upon turning around, he found Fiona standing there with her hands on hips and an accusatory look on her face. A situation that prompted Ralph to ask himself, *What the hell does she want from me now?* Abruptly, she told him they needed to talk, and without waiting for a response, she grabbed his arm and led him to her car. After driving them both to a local pub, she purchased a round of drinks then found a table out of earshot from other patrons. Once seated, Fiona bluntly told Ralph that she was pregnant, and consequently, he had no other choice than to marry her immediately. Having delivered the message, Fiona swallowed the remains of her gin and tonic then swaggered back to her car without uttering another word.

Fiona's mother was upset when she received her daughter's news and was not at all placated by Fiona's attempts to blame

Ralph for her condition. But contrary to what Fiona had initially assumed, her mother's true concern was not for her daughter's well-being or how the situation had come to pass, but rather, what impact the prevailing circumstances may have on the family reputation! Consequently, her focus and energy were geared only toward actions necessary to provide damage control in this area. To implement these considerations, Fiona's father used his considerable influence to organize an immediate church wedding while side-stepping the normal notifications. Additionally, he made arrangements to have a cottage that he owned in a remote part of Cornwall vacated in order that Ralph and Fiona could effectively isolate themselves for a twelve-month period. Two months after the wedding, the family would put out a joyful announcement that Fiona was pregnant, but due to medical complications, she required complete rest. Subsequently, and on the advice of her doctor, she would be residing in a tranquil location and, regrettably, wouldn't be able to receive visitors until she'd fully recovered her strength, which most likely would be after the birth of the baby. This absence would enable the family to select an acceptable date for the child's birth while allowing Fiona to avoid returning into circulation until the baby was several months old. To legitimize this plan of action, the family solicitor would be instructed to take care of any annoying details regarding birth certificates and the like to ensure embarrassments were avoided later in the child's life.

Following a white wedding, an extravagant reception, and a honeymoon in Paris, Fiona and Ralph went directly to the family home in Cornwall where they stayed until their newborn daughter was six months old. On their return to Watford, they moved into a plush three-bedroom apartment that Fiona's parents had purchased, whereupon Fiona hired a nanny. These arrangements allowed her to return to a supervisory role at the manufacturing company and rejoin the social scene she'd engaged in prior to her dalliance with Ralph. Fiona made it clear that she expected Ralph to behave like a faithful husband and loving father at all times while clarifying that such conditions did not necessarily apply to her. The underlying rationale, she explained, was that it was he who had made her pregnant and not the other way around! Furthermore, failure to abide by her rules would result in Ralph being removed from the apartment, fired from his job, and, as far as possible, prevented from ever seeing his daughter again. Ralph was both angry and frustrated at the position he found himself in, but at the same time, he didn't see any other viable options. He knew divorce would be heavily frowned upon by his own parents, and further, losing his daughter was more than he could bear. Given his predicament, he decided to knuckle down and let the future unfold in its own sweet way.

CHAPTER 11

Eight months had passed by since my chance encounter with Ralph. Despite our meetings being largely brief and secretive, I now felt I knew more about him than anyone else in the entire world. There was no doubt we'd fallen madly in love, but we avoided talking about a future together; we subconsciously knew that a meaningful one was simply impractical. Soon however, this reality started to become more than just a mild frustration, as we were obviously perpetuating a fantasy that could only end in bitter disappointment. Additionally, odds were that we'd eventually be spotted by somebody who knew one of us; the consequences of which could be disastrous. Taking all things into account, I now knew beyond any doubt that I needed to make the tough decision to end our relationship once and for all.

Over the next few days, I worked on strengthening my resolve, and by the time our next meeting at the park came around, I'd worked up the courage to initiate our final meeting conversation. Knowing it would almost certainly be a painful event, I planned on getting it over with as quickly as possible. However, My intentions were sidetracked when Ralph greeted me by saying, "Guess what? I've been asked to get the family cottage in Rye ready for summer again. And as Fiona won't be joining me this time, I'd like you to come with me!" At first, I assumed he was joking, but judging by the look on his face, it soon became clear that he wasn't! He went on to tell me that he'd given the matter considerable thought and had devised a plan that would allow it to happen without anyone else knowing. It involved him sending me a fake letter from an imaginary school friend who now lived on the south coast, inviting me to attend the christening of her first child. This, he explained, would provide justification for such a visit, and if my in-laws were willing to take care of Sophie for the weekend, there shouldn't be any reason why I couldn't join him; unless, of course, Paul objected. To add authenticity to the plan, I could have a family member take me to the tube station, as this would give the impression that I was going into Central London to catch a mainline train. Instead, I would get off after a couple of stops, where Ralph would meet me and drive us to our destination. The simplicity of the plan, he summarized, was why it should be successful!

For the very first time in Ralph's presence, I was stunned into silence, and my trance wasn't broken until he asked, "Are you trying to catch flies?"—a jovial reference to my mouth being wide open. His humor helped me relax, but even after organizing my thoughts, I told him the plan was far too audacious, let alone the potential consequences if we were to be caught out. I'd expected that to be the end of the discussion, but it soon became clear that Ralph didn't see things the same way as I did.

"The first step is simple," he said. "You receive the letter and use it to seek permission to attend. Whether such permission is granted or not, what's the risk?" He asked calmly. After nodding to indicate my agreement, Ralph proceeded to run through the rest of his plan again. By this point, he'd pretty much convinced me that if we followed it carefully there was, in fact, little risk. I acknowledged such but emphasized that Paul likely wouldn't go along with the idea anyway; the subject was probably moot. "Well, let's give it a try and see what happens," Ralph concluded with a wide smile. I knew it was only a convenient excuse, but yet again, I managed to convince myself that the prospect of spending a weekend away with Ralph justified delaying the tough conversation that I'd promised myself we'd have—to another day!

*   *   *   *

Four days later, a letter arrived at my house. I opened it to find an invitation from a fictitious Anne Edwards, a name I'd made up on the spot the previous Saturday. That evening, I broached Paul on the subject and showed him the letter. His facial expression conveyed total disinterest, but fortunately, when I was able to assure him that it wouldn't interfere with his plans or cost him any money, he offered no objection. With that hurdle out of the way, I visited my in-laws to explain the situation and ask if Sophie could spend the weekend with them. To my delight, they were agreeable, and from the smile on my face, I think Ralph knew what my answer would be when he walked through the café door the following Tuesday. Feeling the need to control the combination of anxiety and excitement I was experiencing, we decided not to meet again until the day of our planned trip.

That weekend, I went clothes shopping; I wanted to look my best for our weekend away. I couldn't possibly have been more excited; though at the same time, I did have a nagging dread that someone who knew us may discover our plan. And to make matters worse, I now also felt a little guilty about leaving Sophie alone overnight for the first time.

Eventually, the big day arrived. I'd packed my overnight case the previous evening together with a small one for Sophie, and after waking her at six o'clock for breakfast, we set off on the ten-minute walk to my in-laws' house. Having assured my daughter that I'd be back the following evening, my father-in-law gave me a ride on the rear seat of his motorbike to South Harrow tube station, where I waved him goodbye before purchasing my ticket. Standing on the platform, I felt myself relax a little, as the part of the plan I was most concerned about was now behind me. After boarding the next train to arrive, I rode the four stops to Park Royal. There, I disembarked and walked two blocks south before taking a right turn. Hoping I'd remembered the instructions correctly, I was greatly relieved when I saw a blue Morris Minor parked at the curbside with Ralph sitting behind the wheel.

As we took off towards the A21 road, my anxiety evaporated and was replaced with an inner sense of elation. We talked about the upcoming weekend, and in our newfound freedom, the conversation covered subjects we'd never touched on before. Absorbed by the moment, time passed rapidly, and in what seemed little more than a blink of the eye, we passed a signpost that read *Rye 15 miles.*

Shortly before reaching the cottage, Ralph pulled up outside a general store where he purchased the list of stock up items his wife had given him. When we arrived at the cottage, we dropped off the goods then set off on foot to the local fish and chip shop. It may have been the adjacency to the local fishing boats and therefore the freshness of the produce, or perhaps just my frame of mind, but the cod and chips with a side helping of garden peas were the finest I'd ever tasted.

Following lunch, we walked back to the cottage then drove down to the beach. There, we walked along the shoreline, which led to the town center, where we moseyed around several gift shops and other places of interest. We arrived back at the cottage shortly after five o'clock, and as Ralph had made dinner reservations for seven-thirty, we decided to take a short nap prior to getting ourselves suitably dressed.

The restaurant was beautifully decorated with vertically striped wallpaper, and the heart-shaped wall lights gave it a romantic atmosphere. I must say I didn't recognize many of the items on the menu, as I had no previous experience of eating in an establishment of this nature. But with Ralph's help and advice from the waiter, we made our selections. The food was outstanding, the conversation flowed easily, interspersed with hearty laughter, and I wanted the evening to last forever. I hadn't given any thought as to how we would split the bill, and when it came time to leave, I only hoped I had enough money to pay my share, fearing it had been a rather expensive meal. My concern was removed, however, when the waiter came by to thank Ralph, which made me realize he must have settled the account during my visit to the ladies' room. His kindness and thoughtfulness only reinforced what I already knew.

On our arrival back at the cottage, I resisted the urge to dance wildly and scream for joy. When I first agreed to the trip, Ralph had made a point of telling me about the separate sleeping arrangements available in the cottage. I really appreciated his considerate ways, as I knew he wanted to convey that he had no unspoken expectations of me. While I was both comfortable and confident that Ralph wouldn't attempt to do anything that I didn't want him to, my instincts were now telling me that he'd really like to move our relationship another step forward if possible!

After Ralph made tea, we sat together on the sofa, chatting idly. Following a lull in the conversation, he turned towards me and pushed my hair to one side before tucking it behind my neck. Then he kissed my ear while placing a hand on my knee. Slowly, his mouth worked around my face until our lips met. At first, we kissed softly, but the intensity gradually increased as did my level of desire.

When our lips finally parted, Ralph gave me a loving smile before saying, "We should probably make it an early night, Shirley, my dear. That way, we can get up early in the morning and make the most of our time before heading home."

I chewed over Ralph's words wondering whether he was just making a practical suggestion or, perhaps, that he was fishing to see if I had any inclination to join him in his bedroom. I decided that whatever he may be thinking, I was going to leave it entirely up to him to make the move if he so chose.

"Good idea," I said. "I'll go and get myself ready." Hurrying off, I went upstairs to the bathroom where I washed my face, brushed my teeth, and ran a brush through my hair prior to slipping into the silky red nightdress that I'd purchased the previous weekend.

On exiting the bathroom, I found Ralph waiting for me on the landing, wearing a pair of navy-blue pajamas. He wished me goodnight and kissed me softly on my lips, a kiss that slowly grew stronger as he gradually wrapped his arms around my waist, pulling me closer towards him. Aroused to a point where I knew I was starting to lose control, Ralph kissed the nape of my neck before whispering in my ear, "Shall we take this into the bedroom, my darling?" A question I no longer felt needed an answer!

*　*　*　*

With the lights dimmed, Ralph took me in his arms again; then he nibbled on my ear before slowing working his mouth around to my lips. Our kissing quickly became more intense, and soon our tongues were touching playfully. With my mind floating away, I felt Ralph's hand deftly slip under my nightdress before his firm fingers massaged my back in a continuous circular motion. I didn't think it possible to want him more than I did at that moment, but my desire increased yet another notch when he nimbly removed my nightdress and began running his tongue around my protruding nipples, causing my body to shudder from head to toe. Next, Ralph took off his pajamas, lifted me up, and laid me gently on the bed before further exploring my body with both his hands and his lips until we were finally intimately joined as one. Ralph's subsequent pelvic motions were slow but firm, and we moved in perfect unison. When my passion reached a new crescendo, I found myself involuntarily screaming aloud followed by uninhibited groans of satisfaction, reactions I'd never experienced before. With feelings of security while wrapped snuggly in Ralph's arms and comforted by the warmth of his body, I slowly drifted into a wonderfully peaceful sleep.

*   *   *   *

I awoke the next morning with my head resting on Ralph's chest, feeling the rhythmic beating of his heart while, at the same time, listening to his gentle breathing. We'd planned to get up early and walk along the shoreline to enjoy the sea air, but when Ralph stirred, our minds went elsewhere. We made love for the second time, and while I wouldn't have believed it possible, Ralph took me to even greater heights than he had the night before. When our passion finally ended, I must have instantly fallen asleep again because the next thing I remember was being a little startled when Ralph gently touched my shoulder while handing me a cup of tea.

By the time we were washed and dressed, it was past eleven o'clock. Realizing that there wasn't much time left before our journey home, we walked to the beach to stretch our legs. Back at the cottage, I prepared tinned salmon and cucumber sandwiches for our lunch while Ralph tidied up the bathroom. When we finished eating, Ralph washed the dishes, and I made up the bed, and by two o'clock, we were on our way home.

Our journey back was simply delightful. We talked much as we'd always done, but clearly, something new and special had been added to the mix. We found ourselves laughing at silly little things, and at one point, we broke into song. Neither of us had particularly tuneful voices, but that didn't detract from our enthusiasm or the enjoyment we got from giving it all we had to offer. When I sang the wrong words to one particular tune, Ralph laughed so hard he had to pull off the road in order to regain his composure!

Though I was looking forward to seeing Sophie again, in truth, I wished the weekend would never end. Regrettably, the time passed quickly, and sooner than I'd hoped, we were approaching our destination. As an extra precaution against being spotted by anyone who might recognize us, Ralph dropped me off where we'd met the previous morning, and we engaged in one last passionate kiss. After exiting the car with my case in hand, Ralph rolled down the driver's side window and said, "I love you, Shirley." I was still wiping away tears of joy when I arrived at South Harrow Station.

*   *   *   *

While the weekend in Rye was an uplifting experience, it had the unintended consequence of further highlighting my general dissatisfaction with everyday life. Furthermore, it emphasized the urgency of having the tough conversation that I knew I must have with Ralph, which, once again, I'd been putting off! A combination of these pressures began to make me even more irritable, and this state of mind surfaced when I snapped at Sophie for no good reason. Understandably, she was upset, as I'd never behaved that way before. But now I faced another emotion that I really didn't care for; it was called remorse!

Sophie was a little wary of me for the next couple of days, and my attempts at spoiling her were bearing little fruit. Eventually, I did what I should have done in the first place. I apologized, explaining that I was upset at the time though I knew that didn't excuse my behavior. I was fearful that she'd ask what had caused my distress and was prepared to tell a white lie if needs be. Fortuitously, she just smiled and kissed me, saying that she understood, as she'd once said something bad to a friend when she was upset.

The incident with Sophie spurred me into swift action. With a new sense of purpose, I committed myself to reconcile the surreptitious relationship I'd had with Ralph at our very next meeting, no matter what! After all, there were only two options open to us; we could either commit to a life together and deal with the implications or we could call it a day and move on!

*   *   *   *

At our next get-together, I shared my thoughts with Ralph, and frankly, I wasn't surprised to discover they essentially matched his. We discussed the possibility of both seeking divorce, but after reviewing the practicalities of such an action, we came to a disappointing and demoralizing conclusion. Ralph told me that despite Fiona's selfish and uncaring attitude towards motherhood, she'd never, ever, allow their daughter to be in his custody. Furthermore, her parents would use their considerable influence to protect their daughter's wishes, if only to protect the family name. For my part, though, despite trying to convince myself otherwise, I also knew that Paul and his family would fight tooth and nail if I tried to leave with Sophie, and in all probability, they'd succeed.

We'd established earlier in our relationship that neither of us would ever do anything that prevented us from maintaining custody of our children. And given that we could find no feasible way of pursuing a life together that included our offspring, with heavy hearts, we said our final goodbyes.

CHAPTER 12

Three months had passed since my final meeting with Ralph. During that time, I remained focused on the singular goal I'd now set for myself, that being to make my marriage work no matter what it took! To this end, I began reading up on football and Arsenal in particular, and additionally, whenever possible, I joined my husband on his visits to the local pub. Initially, Paul reacted negatively to my efforts, and I frequently found myself the target of his scorn and sarcasm. But I wasn't about to be put off, and if anything, his resistance only increased my resolve. Following several weeks of constant effort on my part, which produced no tangible results, I finally made a small breakthrough one evening at the Coach and Horses pub.

Paul was talking to his friend John about Arsenal's upcoming home game against Chelsea. "Do you think that young stud who's been scoring loads of goals is all he's cracked up to be?" John asked. To which I promptly interjected, "Are you talking about Jimmy Greaves by any chance?" At first, Paul looked dumbfounded; though after gathering himself, he continued to ignore me, much as he usually did in such circumstances. From that point on, however, John began to include me in the conversation, and as the evening wore on, Paul occasionally did as well! When the bell for last orders rang, I felt like I'd at least made some progress, but the cherry on the cake was still to come. On our walk home, Paul put his hand around my waist, something he hadn't done since our courting days!

Following the milestone night at the local pub, I began to notice a new trend slowly develop in both Paul's behavior and attitude. Admittedly, they were mostly minor things, such as saying "hello" and "goodbye" when he came and went, picking up his dirty clothes on occasion, and spending a little more time with our daughter. Though these were all small steps, they were, nevertheless, steps in the right direction!

I continued to be encouraged by my husband's increased attentiveness, and this didn't go unnoticed by others in our circle. "Have you been feeding Paul happy fruit for breakfast lately?" Grace asked one Saturday afternoon when we met for tea.

"Is there any particular reason for asking me that?" I asked, keen to see if she might elaborate.

"Well, for what it's worth, both Billy and I have noticed a change in him recently. He's more talkative and seems in a better mood than I remember him being for a long time." Grace paused for a moment, but with a cheeky smile, she continued, "Of course, Billy thinks it can only be the result of more action in the bedroom!"

"The dirty bugger," I replied laughing along with Grace. "But seriously, Paul has been making an effort to be more of a family man, and I very much appreciate it. Which reminds me, our tenth wedding anniversary is coming up this summer. Do you and Billy have any plans to celebrate it?"

"We've talked about it, but things are a bit tight money wise at the moment. So, most likely we'll just have a party at home. Naturally, you and Paul will be the first couple invited. And though we'll keep things simple, we can still have a lively knees up, which should be fun."

Grace asked if I had any ideas to which I said I hadn't really, but I supposed in a perfect world it would be wonderful if the four of us were able to make a return visit to North Wales, where we'd all spent our honeymoons together. "Of course, that would be fantastic, but regrettably, it's just not practical," she said woefully.

We talked through other possibilities when a thought flashed through my mind, "You know, Grace, the only really expensive part of our honeymoon was the accommodations. What if we went to the same location but camped by the lake rather than staying in the guest house?"

At first, Grace gave me a look I was familiar with; it basically said, "Are you nuts?" But slowly, the look disappeared, and I could tell her mind was working overtime. Suddenly, she blurted out. "You know, this might be one of those rare occasions when you have the inklings of a sensible idea." She pulled a face that let me know her sarcasm was meant in jest. "My uncle has a tent and camping equipment," she added, adopting a more serious tone. "I'm fairly sure he'd let us borrow them if I asked. That would at least be a good start; though even then, I still don't know if we'd be able to afford it."

"Might be worth giving it more thought," I replied, as the idea seemed increasingly appealing to me, and I didn't want to drop the subject without exploring it further. "Another thing that could help is roughing it because we wouldn't need to take so many clothes!" I added, hopefully.

"You're right," Grace said, with a glimmer of enthusiasm. "Given the circumstances, that wouldn't bother me one little bit. Just returning to the same spot after ten long years would be so romantic that little else would matter. I'm sure I'd still have a great time, even if I were only wearing a sack! And surely we could still afford a meal or two at the guest house rather than cooking all the time. Plus, the men could have their beer at the bar. When all's said and done, we have to eat and drink whether we go away or not. And to keep the cost down even further, we could limit the trip to seven days rather than the fourteen we took last time,"

Grace continued, clearly intrigued with the possibility of making the idea real. But after running through all the details we could think of, neither of us was really sure if we were only daydreaming or not. "Let me run it by Billy tonight." Grace finally concluded, "He's good at this sort of thing. Unless he just poo-poos it out of hand, the four of us could meet up tomorrow afternoon to discuss it further."

*   *   *   *

We'd just finished our Sunday lunch when Grace and Billy arrived. It was clear from their demeanor that they were both excited, so I showed them into the living room, anxious to hear what they had to say. "Grace told me your idea for our tenth wedding anniversary," Billy started out. "We both think it would be incredible if we could make it happen, but there are several things that need to be checked out before we can decide if it's feasible or not. I'm going to do some investigation this week, so let's plan on meeting up next weekend to review where we stand."

*   *   *   *

I spent the rest of the week on tenterhooks, as the more I thought about the possibility of returning to Wales for our tenth wedding anniversary, the more excited I became. Finally, Saturday arrived, and as planned, Grace and Billy came to our home in the early afternoon. Both appeared a little cautious when we assembled in our living room, and I wasn't sure how to read their mood. After some idle chatter, Billy took a deep breath while I nervously waited to hear what he had to say.

"Grace and I visited her uncle this week. He told us that we are more than welcome to borrow his camping equipment whenever we want to. Unfortunately, it's quite bulky and very heavy, so together with our respective luggage, I'm not sure if it's practical to haul it all to the train station and load it into a carriage. Even if we were able to, the challenges of getting it off the train, onto the coach, and from there to the campsite, frankly, just aren't achievable."

On hearing Billy's conclusion summary, my heart dropped, and I wanted to cry. The four of us sat in silence until Billy interjected enthusiastically, "Well, that's the bad news, but it's possible there may be another way. At the moment, it's only an outside shot, so don't get your hopes up, as I'd hate for you to end up disappointed." He hesitated for a moment, "I happened to mention the situation to my factory foreman during a tea break last Thursday. At the time, he only listened without responding, but at the end of the workday, he asked me to stay behind for a few minutes." Billy paused and wiped his lips. "He told me he'd relayed our story to the deputy factory manager. Apparently, he was sympathetic and said he'd find out if it were possible for us to use one of the company trucks; though at best, that could only happen on a Saturday or Sunday. I told him that could work for us, as we planned on leaving one weekend and coming back the next. He went on to say the trucks could only be driven by a company certified driver, but given the purpose, he felt confident he'd find a volunteer. He would still need permission from the factory manager and wasn't sure if he'd be able to get that or not, but he would try. So, as I started out saying, it's far from certain this could work for us, but at least it appears to be a possibility."

"Well, thanks for all your efforts, Billy; they're much appreciated. Paul and I totally understand it's not a done deal, but if you don't mind me asking, when might we get a yes or no?" I asked.

"By the end of this week, I think. As I've already said, please don't get your hopes up too high, as there's a chance it won't happen. But you can be assured Grace and I will let you know the moment we do."

* * * *

Each day, I prayed that Billy would stop off on his way home from work with the news that I desperately wanted to hear. But when Wednesday came and went without further word, I started to get despondent. Yes, I knew Billy had made it perfectly clear from the beginning that using the company truck was only a possibility, but I suppose I'd assumed that everything would turn out alright in the end. In an effort to get my mind elsewhere, I took off to the kitchen to start dinner preparations. I'd just finished peeling the potatoes when I heard a knock on our front door, and not expecting anyone to be calling at this time, I asked Paul to answer it. When he did, I heard the familiar voices of Grace and Billy, so I dropped what I was doing and ran to meet them. Billy was trying his best to look serious, but when he saw me, he could no longer contain himself. "We're all going to Wales!" he screamed out, a prelude to the four of us linking arms and dancing wildly around the room.

CHAPTER 13

I'd been marking the days off for what seemed like a lifetime when suddenly we were only one week away from our much-anticipated return trip to Wales. Grace and I had prepared a list of the items we needed to take for our upcoming adventure, and following a few frantic days of shopping, washing, ironing, cooking and packing, we were finally ready. On Friday evening, I made an early dinner for Sophie before dropping her off at my in-laws where she would be staying during our time away. When I arrived back home, Paul and I ran over our checklist before getting an early night, knowing we had to be up at the crack of dawn the next morning.

Jumping out of bed on the sound of our alarm clock buzzing, I cooked breakfast and then cleared up the dishes while Paul took our luggage out to the street. As planned, the company truck arrived at precisely 6:30 am, and after loading our cases, we set off to Grace's house where she and Billy were waiting at curbside with their luggage and the camping equipment packed and ready. Minutes later, we were all set, and before the clock struck 7:30 am, we were on our way.

George Cummins, the driver who'd volunteered to chauffeur us, was a likeable individual with a great sense of humor. And within minutes of our journey beginning, he had us all in stitches. He told us that he was keen to get back home before midnight, and if we didn't mind, he'd be putting his foot down when it was safe to do so. "Not a problem, mate, provided you don't jeopardize the valuable goods sitting in the back seat," Billy said with a chuckle, pointing at Grace and myself. To further help George's wishes, we only made a couple of short stops to use the bathroom and utilized that time to make tea and eat the sandwiches we'd previously prepared. The journey went smoothly, and we reached our destination shortly after two o'clock, nearly an hour earlier than originally anticipated. On arrival, we unloaded all of our belongings then treated George to lunch, waving him goodbye forty-five minutes later. While we'd all enjoyed his company, we hoped it would feel like a long way off before we saw him again!

*   *   *   *

I'd mentally prepared myself to cope with any unexpected challenges that camping threw at me; I was determined not to let any such inconveniences spoil our much-anticipated holiday celebration. To my surprise and delight, the whole experience was turning out to be much more fun than I'd imagined. Cooking meals was, of course, limited by the basic equipment we had available though that in itself led to plenty of laughs. Perhaps the biggest concern both Grace and I shared revolved around the washing and toilet facilities, but we had a stroke of luck in that department. On our first evening, we visited the guest house where we'd stayed ten years previously, in order that the men could have a beer. To our amazement, the establishment had the same manager as on our previous visit, and he recognized us immediately. "Good evening, ladies. Welcome back. To what do I owe this honor?" He said in a jovial manner.

"We're celebrating our tenth wedding anniversary," I replied.

"Ten years! That can't possibly be true! You don't look a day older than the last time I saw you!" he responded with a smile that stretched from one ear to the other.

"Flattery will get you *anywhere!*" Grace replied, picking up on the banter. "Actually, it's nothing short of a miracle that we're here at all. We both have kids now, so naturally, money is a bit tight. But we all loved staying in this area so much, we figured that we'd have to visit again come hell or high water. Unfortunately, the only way we could manage that was by roughing it in a tent!" Grace said while pushing her nose up with her index finger and pointing towards the campsite.

"Will we be getting the pleasure of your company for dinner one evening, perhaps?" the manager asked.

"You most certainly will. Wednesday is our actual anniversary date, so we'll be here that evening for sure," I chimed in, recollecting how delicious the food was the last time we were here.

"Then, ladies, I'll make sure you have a table with the very best view of the lake. And by the way, if either of you want to use our staff bathroom or toilet facilities, just ask the receptionist. I'll make sure she knows that I've authorized you to do so."

"Thank you very, very, much", Grace and I said in unison, grateful that a potential concern had now been eliminated; though privately, I still failed to understand why the men seemed to be actually looking forward to a week absent personal hygiene!

Following four delightful days of walking and revisiting local sites, we set off to our dinner treat at the guest house. On arrival, we were escorted to an outside table, which afforded us a beautiful view of the adjacent lake. Both the men ordered beers, so Grace and I treated ourselves to a glass of sherry, something we rarely did. We spent ages looking over the menu, and by the time we'd selected our meals, the men were already on their second pint!

The food was even better than I remembered, and if that wasn't enough, the waiter gave us a wonderful surprise. When he came to collect our plates, he told us the manager was giving us a fifty percent discount on the bill as an anniversary gift! While

Grace and I were extremely grateful for his generosity, the men saw it as a reason to order more beer, and given the circumstances, we didn't much mind.

We sat and talked for a while before Grace and I ordered ice cream for dessert, and the men ordered more drinks. The sun was beginning to set, transforming the lake's grey surface into shimmering reflections of red and gold. The view put me in a romantic mood, and the memory of Paul taking me for a boat ride across the lake on our previous visit came to mind. The guest house had several rowboats that its occupants could use whenever they wished, so on my way back from a bathroom visit, I asked the manager if we could possibly use one this evening. He was so gracious, saying, "Of course, my dear, anytime you like."

When I returned to our table, I asked Paul if he'd row me across the lake, as I'd like to lay back and watch the stars that were getting brighter and more spectacular by the minute. I could tell by the look on his face that he wasn't overly keen on the idea, but egged on by Billy, he reluctantly agreed, only of course, after ordering two more cans of beer to take with him.

On our way to the lake's edge, I noticed Paul was swaying slightly, and his speech was a little slurred though, over the years, he'd learned how to handle himself when drinking significant quantities of alcohol. In any event, I wasn't particularly worried about his condition, as, after all, I knew I could easily row us both back safely if need be. We pushed the boat into the water before jumping in ourselves, and Paul started rowing at one end while I reclined at the other, watching the magic of the night sky unfold before my eyes.

We were about halfway across the lake when I asked Paul if we could stop for a while in order to take in our beautiful surroundings. He stopped immediately, but his motivation wasn't the view; rather, he saw it as an opportunity to open a can of beer. I'm guessing we'd been stationary for about ten or fifteen minutes when I suggested we may want to turn around and head back to shore. "Just wait until I've finished my beer," he replied, moments prior to my hearing the second can being opened. While I knew Paul had a large capacity to hold his alcohol, he had consumed five or six pints and now almost of two additional cans, so it came as no surprise when he announced in a loud voice that he needed to relieve himself. Those, of course, were not his actual words; rather, "I need a fucking piss" were closer to his mutterings. Paul always had a tendency to use foul language when he'd had a lot to drink, and I supposed I'd got used to it even if I didn't approve of his vulgarity.

In the process of standing up and unzipping his fly, Paul staggered, causing the boat to rock quite violently from side to side. "Careful," I called out anxiously, "or you may tip us over." I sensed Paul was no longer in full control of his actions, and I instinctively knew it was time for me to start taking charge. "Why don't you kneel down and pee over the side? Then come to this end of the boat and lay down. I'm happy to row us back to shore," I called out.

"I know what I'm fucking doing!" he shouted back. "Do you think I'm bloody stupid or something?" On hearing his response, I knew I needed to take action quickly before something unfortunate happened. I pleaded with Paul to pee carefully and then sit down while we exchanged places. Regretfully, this hit the wrong nerve, and I could tell he was getting increasingly angry. He cursed while jumping onto the platform he'd been sitting on, causing the boat to again sway rapidly to one side. Miraculously, he managed to maintain his balance until the boat swayed back in the other direction, throwing him headfirst into the water.

I screamed at the sight I'd just witnessed until I realized panicking wouldn't help, and I had to do something positive. I picked up one of the oars and held it over the side, thinking it would enable Paul to grab hold of it and climb back into the boat. But as my eyes adjusted to the darkness of the water, I could see no trace of him. I knew Paul wasn't much of a swimmer but assumed he must have somehow maneuvered himself into a different spot from the one he'd fallen into. Carefully, I worked my way around the perimeter of our boat, when suddenly I saw his head appear. I held the oar in his direction, sure that by grabbing it, he would be able to climb safely back on board, but in an instant, he disappeared again. Certain he'd soon resurface, I waited, telling myself to be patient.

But I never saw him again.

CHAPTER 14

(AUGUST 1963—INVERNESS)

After allowing me to collect my handbag and lock the front door, Constable McFarland directed me to sit in the back seat of his vehicle before taking off to the local police station. I asked for the second time if he could explain to me what was happening and why I'd been arrested. "Surely there must be some mistake," I pleaded, but again there was no response. Though I was certain there had to be some misunderstanding taking place, I found myself becoming a little scared, as nothing about my situation was making any sense.

On our arrival, I was taken to a small room and left alone for more than twenty minutes. Suddenly, the door swung open, and a slim bald-headed officer accompanied by a young woman wearing a navy-blue suit appeared. The gentleman sat in the seat opposite mine and introduced himself as Detective Inspector McKay while the woman sat at the end of the table in silence. Detective inspector McKay proceeded to ask questions in relation to Paul's accident, all of which appeared routine, and during this time, the woman took notes. With the question period apparently over, the detective inspector pulled a sheet of paper from his briefcase and stared at me before saying, "Mrs. Harris, you are hereby charged with first-degree murder."

I'm not sure if he said anything further, as the next thing I remember was regaining consciousness while lying on a sofa in the police station rest area. The following day, I was put into the rear portion of a police transport vehicle and driven to North West London where I was transferred into a small holding cell.

* * * *

Out of nowhere and for no apparent reason, my life began to take on a surreal nature, and every moment felt like a nightmare that had no ending. My days were spent either in solitude or partaking in lengthy meetings with my assigned legal counsel. Finally, following close to six months of incarceration, the date of my trial arrived, and at 10 am on a Wednesday morning, I appeared at the magistrate's court.

CHAPTER

(JANUARY 1963—HARROW)

When Detective Inspector Mark Redman arrived at his office on Tuesday morning, he was greeted by the usual pile of paperwork. Like most in his line of business, he disliked the desk side of the job, and though he knew that most of the required reading was simply red tape, he was aware that there was always the possibility of finding a useful snippet of information. Having worked his way through the official stack of communications and circulars, he moved onto the internal daily report. This was a handwritten document prepared by the on-duty officer that summarized information received from members of the public the previous day. Reading this report invariably provided Mark with a few chuckles, and he often saved parts of it to share with close colleagues, knowing it would likely amuse them too. He'd long since believed that the vast majority of the crazy and far-fetched things people would say they'd seen or heard could only be provided by local crackpots or loners with nothing better to do. Notwithstanding this, Mark knew that reading the report was his duty to the public, and he wasn't going to let them down. Today's list was the normal gibberish though, for some reason, information provided by an elderly woman did catch his eye.

It didn't accuse anyone of a specific crime, which alone made it unusual but rather said the circumstances surrounding the issue were so fishy that she felt an investigation was warranted. He very much doubted this, but for reasons he wouldn't have readily been able to put into words, the report intrigued him. Mark glanced at his watch. He had two hours to kill before his next meeting, and as the woman who'd given the report lived only five minutes away, he decided to pay her a quick visit.

*   *   *   *

Moments after Detective Inspector Redman knocked on the door of 54 Shepherds Terrace, a stout lady with dark brown hair tied in a bun appeared in the doorway. She looked him up and down while asking, "How can I help you, young man?" Mark showed her his identification badge and explained the reason for his call.

Mark was a seasoned professional who knew the ropes. Much of his questioning was geared toward finding out what type of person Mrs. Hoskins was rather than digging into the story she'd reported. He knew this would most likely be the determining factor as to whether or not he'd devote any further time to the matter.

At the conclusion of a forty-five-minute discussion, Mark's instincts told him that Mrs. Hoskins was almost certainly of sound mind and not a vindictive person. Also, he had to agree that on the surface, at least, what she had relayed did appear very fishy. Though at the same time, Mrs. Hoskins acknowledged that her observation only offered proof that a trustworthy individual had made a statement she knew to be untrue. Initially, Mark concluded that there was no reason to spend further time on a matter of no known consequence, but later in the day, he decided he'd follow up further if time permitted.

*   *   *   *

Having just downed his fourth pint of best bitter, Detective Inspector Redman knew it was time for him to go home. Given the hours he'd put in recently to conclude a particularly nasty armed robbery case, he didn't feel obliged to arrive at the office early the next morning or be in tip-top form. But at the same time, he'd reached the stage in life where dealing with a hangover normally outweighed the enjoyment he got from the process of acquiring one.

The following morning Mark returned to working his way through his paperwork backlog; though when noon arrived, he hadn't even reached the halfway mark. In an attempt to clear his head, he decided to go for a walk, hoping it would put him in a better frame of mind and enable him to make more headway with the pile that appeared to resist getting smaller. But when he returned to his desk, he simply wasn't in the right mood. Rather than fret about it, he resolved to change gears, get an early night, and hopefully come in with a better attitude the following day. While considering how to make the best use of the remainder of the afternoon, his mind drifted back to his meeting with Mrs. Hoskins. He read his notes again to find the names and addresses of the two friends she'd mentioned, and three hours later, he had no doubt that Mrs. Hoskins had, indeed, reported honestly and without prejudice. Notwithstanding his conclusion, there was still no evidence to indicate or even suggest that anything untoward had taken place, so consequently, there could be no justification for the matter to take up further police time.

Mark had learned from experience that it was imperative to change course when you found yourself going down a blind alley, leaving him bemused as to why the Ada Hoskins story continued to gnaw away at him!

* * * *

"Do you have time for me today, boss?" the deputy inspector asked Mark Redman on his return from lunch.

"Sure, take a seat," Mark said without looking up and at the same time regretting his knee-jerk decision to have his deputy take another look at the Mrs. Hoskins matter.

The directions he'd given were typical of most investigations into family matters for he knew it was fundamentally important to understand the relationship between the parties prior to revealing any possible crime that may have been committed. Failure to do this often led to deliberate roadblocks if certain individuals weren't prepared to cooperate or, worse still, if they intentionally misled an investigation.

The brief Mark received from his young assistant was clear and comprehensive. This made him smile inwardly, as he always felt a sense of pride when a team member who he'd personally trained demonstrated good police work. In spite of the update, Mark found himself continuing to vacillate on the subject. As he gave the matter more thought, the message his supervisor put forth at every six-month performance review sprang to mind. "Mark, nobody has a lock on all knowledge. An important part of my job is to offer assistance and advice. But don't think that means I have all the answers either because I can assure you that I don't! That being said, remember the old saying 'two heads are better than one'? So what am I getting at, Mark? It's quite simple, really. If you want to run something by me, then just do it! Never let your ego get in the way of utilizing the resources you have available to you. And remember, I'm here to support you not to find fault with what you're doing."

* * * *

When Detective Inspector Redman had finished relaying his Ada Hoskins story, his boss leaned back in his chair, lit a cigarette, and blew a stream of smoke into the air. "I must say, Mark, your tale does sound rather intriguing. However, given that we haven't received a complaint, it's not really a police matter."

Chief Inspector Hugh Murray held Mark in high regard, but in this instance, he sensed that his detective was simply fascinated by a harmless puzzle that he'd been unable to solve. Nevertheless, he knew Mark's instincts had often proved correct in the past, and he didn't completely overlook that.

"Let me make some calls, and we'll talk again in a week or so," he finally said, without much enthusiasm. Based on Mark Redman's past experience, he believed that his chief's closing remark was just a polite way of saying that nothing further should or would be done, a decision he was happy to accept as he had many other pressing matters to deal with, and he'd already wasted his and other people's valuable time on the subject.

*   *   *   *

Detective Inspector Redman was wrapping up an internal staff meeting when the receptionist handed him a note that read, *The boss is on the line for you.*

Mark promptly returned to his desk and picked up the receiver, "How can I help you, Chief?"

"I'm calling about the Mrs. Hoskins report. I've made a few phone calls, and while I have nothing of substance to tell you, I share your hunch that there may be something to this—even if I haven't been able to figure out what that something is!" The chief chuckled before adding, "I suggest you take another look. But don't give it too much time, Mark, because if anyone else discovers what we're spending time on these days, both you and I will likely end up being carted off in straight jackets."

When Mark hung up, he was still laughing heartily. He truly hoped that one day he would aspire to the level of humility that his boss always demonstrated while recognizing that, far too often, this quality was judged by some as a weakness.

CHAPTER 16

After getting the okay from his superior officer to continue investigating the possible implications of the Ada Hoskins report, Mark Redman considered his next moves.

First of all, he phoned his counterpart in Wales, hoping he'd get a firsthand briefing on any pertinent findings arising from the Paul Weller drowning death inquiry. While the officer in charge said there was nothing that would indicate foul play, he did find a couple of oddities. "It struck me as rather strange that a woman would ask her husband to take her for a boat ride when she knew he was intoxicated. Additionally, she said her husband only surfaced once after falling into the lake. In my experience, when someone is floundering in the water, they normally surface several times even if they can't swim well."

Next, Mark met with Ada Hoskins and one of her longtime friends, Vera Andrews. Vera turned out to be a shy individual, and while possibly in failing health, Mark felt sure she still had all her marbles intact. Several weeks prior, Vera's only son, Billy, had arranged a 70th birthday party for her at his home. It was only a small affair with just Vera's closest friends and family in attendance. During the party, Billy's wife, Grace, gave Ada a brief tour of the house, and in the process, she described the particulars of a photograph hanging on the parlor wall. From this, Ada picked up on a sharp contradiction to something she knew for certain. Not wishing to cause any embarrassment for her friend's daughter-in-law, however, she chose to remain silent, but later that week, she mentioned her observation to Vera. At first, Vera couldn't understand why her friend felt the subject even worthy of discussion, and furthermore, questioned Ada as to the certainty of the identification she claimed to have made, especially as it had taken place several years prior.

Ada was adamant that she never forgot a face, and while what she'd witnessed didn't necessarily mean anything untoward had taken place, she couldn't reconcile the matter in her mind. Why, after all, would a reliable, upstanding young woman make a statement that she knew to be untrue? And naturally, as a result, she found the matter to be highly suspicious.

Because of her desire to avoid controversy within the family, Vera changed the topic of conversation. But later that evening, she found herself mulling over Ada's observations.

Two days later, when taking tea with her daughter-in-law, Vera took the opportunity to casually ask about the photograph Ada had referred to. And the following day, Vera visited Ada, where they mutually agreed that something just didn't add up!

*   *   *   *

Back at his desk, Detective Inspector Redman mused over his findings to date. While he had established a few facts that could be relevant, he was acutely aware that he sadly lacked any evidence of a crime taking place. Additionally, he knew his boss had only given him a limited amount of time to investigate the matter and would undoubtedly expect it to be dropped if nothing concrete was forthcoming in the near future.

Thinking about possible next moves, Mark decided it may be helpful to find out more about James Harris.

*   *   *   *

Tracking the past and present life of James Harris involved phone calls to his past employer, two former work associates, the Inverness police station, and the mother of his deceased wife. From these inquiries, James appeared to be a model citizen whose first wife was killed in a freak accident while on vacation. Mark also spoke to his opposite number, who'd investigated the accident. From this conversation, he discovered that James' wife had been alone at the time of her death while James had been at work, some seventy miles away, a fact that had been corroborated by several of his co-workers.

Lack of meaningful progress was beginning to undermine Mark's usual enthusiasm, and this made him wonder if hanging on to his hunch was nothing short of misguided stubbornness. Knowing that he had several days of outstanding vacation, he decided to check out and spend the rest of the week fishing.

* * * *

When Mark returned to the office, he felt rested and rearing to go though, in truth, he wasn't really sure in which direction! Not being one to give up easily, he still wanted to take the initiative before his boss instructed him to abandon ship.

One last effort, he told himself as he set about carefully rereading the notes that he'd previously prepared on the Hoskins report. At the end of his review, however, he still hadn't found anything worth revisiting. Not one to normally take time out for lunch, Mark surprised himself when, on the spur of the moment, he accepted an offer from a colleague to join him for a pint at the local pub.

* * * *

Having analyzed Arsenal's prospects for the coming season, the two detectives' conversation inevitably turned back to work.

"How's the Hoskins' case coming along, Mark?" Detective Inspector Mike Jones asked. He hadn't heard much about it lately though, largely because of that, he guessed things probably weren't going that well.

"To be perfectly honest, Mike, I've come to a dead end. A few weeks ago, I was quite sure my hunch would prove to be accurate even though it was totally bizarre. But every road I've been down has led me to a dead end."

Mike had been on many cases where extensive investigations had simply fizzled out, and he knew how infuriating that could be. With this in mind, he encouraged Mark to talk about his efforts to date, hoping it might relieve his co-worker's angst and, perhaps, give him renewed inspiration. For the next forty-five minutes, which included the consumption of two more pints, Mark recapped his work. "Well, that's about it," he finally concluded. "I was toying with the idea of meeting the friends of Shirley who were present at the time of Paul's death, but given they've already provided detailed statements, that would be clutching at straws to say the least!"

"One never knows, old chap!" Mike replied chirpily. "Remember what they taught us at the academy! It's often the last place you think of looking that turns out being the most helpful."

*   *   *   *

On his return, Mark found himself thinking about his own future. He'd wanted to be in the police force since the age of twelve, and all in all, he thought his career to date had been quite successful. At the same time, he wondered if he was starting to lose it because in the last two years he'd worked on several cases that had eventually been abandoned, and it looked likely this was about to happen again! Trying to dismiss the pessimistic views that were, regrettably, becoming more prominent, his mind flashed back to Mike's last remark during lunch.

* * * *

Following an unannounced afternoon call at the Andrews' home, Mark returned for the 6:30 pm appointment that he'd arranged with Grace and Billy. There, they met in the front parlor, as Grace had requested the meeting be out of earshot from her children. Mark opened the discussion by emphasizing his visit was purely routine and only necessary to close the books on an old case. He hoped this introduction would help his audience relax, as they appeared to be on edge.

When Mark went on to politely ask if either Grace or Billy could briefly recount the events leading up to Paul Weller's death, Grace began to cry.

Billy reacted immediately, saying coldly, "Why on earth do we have to go through all this crap again?" with his eyes narrowing. He added, "Are you just trying to upset my wife? We've told the police everything we know, time and time again. It's been more than three years since this tragedy took place. Why can't you just let sleeping dogs lie for Christ's sake?"

Mark was neither surprised nor upset by Billy's outburst. He'd seen it all before, and he knew that he'd likely react the same way if the tables were turned.

"Believe me, Billy, I understand where you're coming from. I'd probably say exactly the same thing if I were in your shoes."

Following a few moments of silence, Billy said in a softer voice, "I'm sorry; I didn't mean to fly off the handle, inspector, but even after all this time, it's still a very sad memory, especially for my wife."

Sensing the need to change the tone, Mark asked Grace about her friendship with Shirley. Once Grace had regained her composure, she started telling stories dating back to her youth, and within minutes, she found herself laughing at some of them. Mark knew he'd now created the atmosphere he was looking for, so he kept silent until Grace had worked her way through to the time of the ten-year wedding anniversary accident. At that point, Grace turned to her husband and asked what he remembered about that terrible night. By now, Billy had also relaxed, and his response was a rather jovial, "Why are you asking me? Remember, both Paul and myself were hammered when he and Shirley took off that evening."

Grace took on a serene look. "I must say that I never really did understand why Shirley wanted Paul to take her on the lake when he was in that condition. However, as it had been such a romantic evening, I suppose the moment just felt right for her."

Mark sensed he might be on to something, "Was Shirley normally a careful individual?" he asked.

"Yes, very much so," Grace replied. "She'd never do anything out of the ordinary unless, of course, I really pushed her to." Grace appeared to be caught up in her own thoughts before adding, "I suppose that's why Billy and I were so flabbergasted when out of the blue, she decided to move to Scotland."

Grace's last statement grabbed Mark's full attention though he cautioned himself against jumping in too quickly; he knew that it was better to allow his audience the opportunity to continue talking. Minutes later, Mark got his reward when Grace pointed to a photograph of Shirley and James Harris hanging on the wall. "We thought Shirley was out of her mind when she took off to Inverness and assumed she'd return within weeks. But she got lucky and met the man of her dreams!" Grace said with her eyes welling up again.

Mark knew from his conversation with Billy's mother that both her son and Grace were unaware of Ada Hoskins' observation. His instincts told him it was now time to reveal more information on that particular matter. "Grace, did you know that during the birthday party you held for Billy's mother, one of her friends said you contradicted knowledge she had regarding that photograph?" Mark said, pointing to the far wall.

Graced frowned. "Really? I'm sorry, but I've no idea what you're talking about!"

Mark explained the background and the subsequent statements that were made to the police while avoiding mentioning Ada Hoskins by name.

"May I ask who said that?" Grace asked inquisitively.

"Unfortunately, I'm not at liberty to tell you," Mark said, hoping this wouldn't offend Grace and change her cooperative mood.

"I suppose it doesn't really matter though I can't stand busybodies! In any event, whoever it was got it all wrong. I can personally assure you that Shirley had never met James Harris before responding to his advertisement."

Mark wanted to press the matter further, but at the same time, he didn't want to imply any mistrust. "I don't doubt your word, Grace, but is it just possible that she didn't mention him to you?'

"Not a chance! Shirley told me everything! She's always done that since we were both youngsters. As I said earlier, I was like her big sister, and she always confided in me," Grace said bluntly, clearly annoyed by Mark's insinuation.

Mark wanted to keep the conversation flowing, but picking up on Grace's reaction, he decided to steer it in a different direction. "How did Shirley react after Paul's passing, and do you think that had anything to do with her moving to Scotland?"

"Naturally, Shirley was very upset as we all were," Grace started out. "I think the close relationship she had with her daughter helped though I suspect the loss of her husband was always at the forefront of her mind. Regarding her move to Scotland, that was something else! Both Billy and I were certain she'd never go through with it, but it turned out we were wrong! It all happened so quickly, I'm surprised she managed to get everything organized in time."

Billy nodded his agreement before adding, "Well, almost everything."

Grace gave her husband a puzzled look. "What do you mean by that?"

"Have you forgotten? When Shirley left her house, the council carried out an inspection before the next tenant was allowed in. They found a couple of boxes in the attic that Shirley had forgotten about."

"Oh, that's right; I remember now," Grace chimed in.

"Do you happen to know where those boxes are now?" Mark asked.

"They were taken to Paul's parents' house. I did write and let Shirley know, but I'm not sure if she ever did anything about it."

Mark continued to listen while Grace talked about the communications she'd had with Shirley since her move though his focus was now elsewhere.

CHAPTER 17

When the judge agreed to hear the Shirley Harris case, Detective Inspector Mark Redman felt himself relaxing for the first time in more than six months, much of which had been a very frustrating experience. While the final outcome remained in the balance, he was thrilled that he'd finally been able to submit a case deemed credible. Knowing it might turn into a lengthy process, he decided to take a week's vacation in Cornwall, as that would help him relax in preparation for the long hours that lay ahead.

To make his trip more enjoyable, Mark invited Patsy James to join him. He'd been dating Patsy for the best part of five years, following their first chance meeting at a charity dinner. In the early days, Mark was quite sure the relationship would eventually become a permanent one. But largely due to a combination of long work hours and travel commitments, a traditional marriage never quite fitted their lifestyles. Irrespective, Mark knew that there was probably another unspoken reason for him not popping the question.

At a colleague's birthday party, he'd inadvertently overheard a mutual friend say, "You and Mark have been seeing each other for a long time now, Patsy. So, kindly tell me, when in the hell are you going to tie the knot?"

To which Patsy responded through a seductive smile, "Well, it's like this, you see. As you know, I'm extremely fond of Mark, and we get along famously. So, why would I want to screw up a good thing by marrying him?"

At the time, Mark was certain the remark had only been made in jest. But on further reflection, he'd concluded that it might, indeed, be best to leave things just the way they were.

*   *   *   *

Lying on a deserted sandy Cornwall beach, Mark took the opportunity to discreetly admire Patsy's outrageously gorgeous long legs as she dozed in a deck chair wearing only a slinky teal bikini. While he'd largely enjoyed an open and uninhibited relationship with Patsy, he'd never divulged what it was about her that had originally caught his attention, that being a clear view of the goods on display when she was wearing an evening gown with a side slit that left little to the imagination!

Gradually, Mark found his mind drifting away from one of Patsy's many attributes and, instead, turning towards the recent events and wondering if they'd eventually add up to a conviction. For sure, his efforts had been floundering until his meeting with Grace and Billy Andrews, and while their initial discussion hadn't revealed anything of great importance, it had opened new avenues to pursue—one of which was a meeting with Grace that brought forth further information she'd apparently been unwilling to give with Billy present.

*   *   *   *

Mark had been pleasantly surprised when he found out Mrs. Weller not only had the boxes Shirley Harris had mistakenly left behind but that she was more than willing to hand them over. His attempt at reviewing the contents, however, left him disappointed, as initially they didn't appear to reveal anything of interest. But during a subsequent review, he spotted a date in an old diary that was circled several times in green ink and a note beneath it that read *D. Day.* This finding aroused Mark's curiosity, but he couldn't connect the date or the adjacent notation to any relevant fact. On reaching this conclusion, he realized that he was again grasping at straws. "Cut out the wishful thinking and focus on the facts," he muttered to himself, fearful that he was simply becoming irrational.

Despondent, Mark began packing up the files when, by chance, he happened to notice the cover of the coroner's report, detailing the death of James Harris' wife. There was something about the date that struck a chord with him though, at first, he couldn't figure out why. He was about to continue with the packing when suddenly the penny dropped. The date Shirley had circled in her diary was the same day that James Harris' wife had been killed! Mark had always been highly suspicious of coincidences, and this one was no exception.

CHAPTER 18

(AUGUST 1963—INVERNESS)

Having dropped off his daughters, James Harris hurried back home, as he'd promised to take his wife for lunch. When he pulled into his street, he was surprised to find a black van parked outside his house with a uniformed policeman standing beside it.

"Can I help you, officer?" James asked, after disembarking from his car.

"Are you James Harris?" the officer asked.

"Yes, I am. Has something happened to my wife?" James asked nervously.

"I'm not here to discuss your wife," the officer replied sternly. "I have a warrant for your arrest."

*　*　*　*

On his arrival at the Inverness police station, James Harris was taken to a holding room. There, he was read his rights. Following that, he was allowed to meet with legal counsel, who briefed him on the next steps. While James was interested in what his designated counsel had to say, he was far keener to know what had happened to his wife, a subject that his counsel promised to obtain a status report on as soon as possible.

CHAPTER 

(NORTH WEST LONDON)

When the presiding judge finished calling his courtroom to order, legal counsel for the prosecution took the floor and proceeded to give their opening statements. With this out of the way, the judge ordered a brief recess, during which time my counsel advised me to take notes when we returned to hear the prosecution witnesses.

Following cross-examination of a witness who only provided background information, an elderly woman with dark brown hair tied in a bun was sworn in.

"Have you ever visited Scotland?" the prosecutor asked her firmly.

"No, I've never been there," was the equally firm response.

The prosecutor then handed the witness a photograph, copies of which had already been distributed to the judge, the jury, and me. "Have you ever seen the couple in this picture?" the prosecutor asked with his head tilted to one side.

"Yes, I've seen them on many occasions," Ada Hoskins replied through a faint smile.

At this point, my counsel passed me a handwritten note that asked, *Do you recognize this woman?* I scribbled down, *No, I've never set eyes on her before;* whereupon my counsel leaned over and whispered in my ear, "Clearly a crank, or maybe just mistaken identity; however, I'm going to ask the judge for a ten-minute recess so we can talk things over."

The judge appeared reluctant and somewhat irritated at my counsel's request but begrudgingly granted it.

While we were in the process of picking up our notes, the security guard was helping Ada Hoskins step down from the witness box. He was holding her arm and leading her towards the waiting room, which required them to pass the table we'd been sitting at, and at that very moment, something caused Mrs. Hoskins to slip. While the guard responded quickly enough to stop her from having a nasty fall, it didn't prevent the wig she was wearing from sliding backwards, revealing a head covered in thin, wispy grey hair.

* * * *

"Are you okay, Shirley?" my counsel asked when we arrived back in the office allotted to the defense team. "I don't mean to sound inappropriate, but you look like you've seen a ghost. Is this, by chance, something to do with the testimony from Ada Hoskins? If it is, we need to discuss it right now."

It took me a while to recover my composure, and when I did, I offered an explanation that wasn't true, "No, it had nothing to do with her testimony. It's just that I came over a little faint. That's happened to me several times over the last few months. I'm not exactly sure why. Perhaps it's because of the pressure I've been experiencing since this whole nightmare began."

"Would you like me to arrange for you to see a doctor?" he asked, showing more emotion than he'd displayed since our first meeting.

"That won't be necessary. I'm already starting to feel a little better, and a good night's sleep will probably do the trick."

* * * *

Somehow, I managed to make it through the afternoon session though I had trouble concentrating. I frequently sat with my mind wandering rather than listening to what the prosecution and their witnesses had to say.

It came as a great relief when the judge finally called an end to the day's proceedings; following which, I was escorted back to the holding cell where I'd spend the night.

* * * *

The following morning I met my counsel two hours prior to the trial resuming. During his briefing, I found it difficult to focus, and frankly, increasingly disinterested in what he had to say. It didn't take long for him to pick up on my disposition. "Shirley, are you paying attention? You do realize your future is at stake, don't you?" he asked, while staring at me over the top of his half-moon glasses.

I wanted to say, "What future?" but instead, I told him my mind was elsewhere, as I couldn't stop worrying about what was happening to my husband, James.

The stern expression on my counsel's face slowly melted until it took on a fatherly look, and with his voice softening, he said, "Shirley, I thought it best to avoid that subject until the trial is over. However, on reflection, perhaps it would be better if I informed you of the news I was given last week…"

CHAPTER 20

Left alone in the confines of a small holding cell and following consultation with my legal counsel, I took pen and paper and scribed the following:

To:The Magistrate's Court, their presiding representative/s and whomever the foregoing institution and authorized individuals deem appropriate.

My name is Mrs. Shirley Ann Harris. I'm of sane mind and writing this letter is entirely of my own free will and choice.

I was born in Harrow, Middlesex, on July 16th, 1931, where I lived with my parents in a two-bedroom apartment they rented from the local government.

My childhood was largely an unhappy one, though the singular exception to this was time spent with a girl named Grace.

Upon leaving school, I assumed I'd find more happiness in my life, which hopefully would include meeting a nice boy and starting a loving relationship. Regrettably, my tedious and uneventful life continued; though eventually, Grace did match me up with a friend of the boy she was dating whose name was Paul. From that point on, the four of us spent most of our free time together. I should add at this juncture that I was never in love with Paul, and, in all candor, I only continued the relationship because it appeared to be a better option than being on my own.

One day, Grace told me that she was going to marry her boyfriend, Billy, and sincerely hoped Paul and I would join them in a double wed-

ding. She went on to say that Billy had talked privately with Paul, and he had indicated a willingness to be my husband if he was asked! As one would expect, I was shocked and upset by Grace's implied assumption, let alone being required to do the asking! At the same time, I knew that in her heart, she was only trying to look out for me as she'd always done.

At first, I didn't respond to Grace, as I was too angry to talk. But after cooling down, I considered the matter further. There was little doubt in my mind that marrying Paul was not a wise choice; though the more I thought about it, the alternative seemed even worse. Finally, I managed to persuade myself that if I worked at it, things would be okay. And while I still harbored a degree of reluctance, I agreed to be part of the proposed double wedding.

Despite my decision, I was still uncomfortable and nervous at the wedding ceremony, but by that time, there seemed to be no way of turning back.

As weeks of married life ticked by, I became increasingly unhappy, and my worst nightmare started to become a reality. And in a matter of months, I was at my wit's end.

Falling further and further into a state of despair, something unexpected happened that significantly brightened my mood. I discovered I was pregnant! Though my marriage was still basically an unhappy one, having a daughter brought joy to my life, and this state of mind continued until she started school. Of course, she remained a joy when we were together, but now that I had spare time on my hands, part of my existence became a drudge again. It was during this period that I accidentally came across a part-time job opportunity. Thinking this would help fill in my days as well as provide a little extra cash, I followed up, and fortunately, I landed the position.

My life was now just about bearable. However, I still sorely lacked the love and affection of a partner that I'd yearned for since my early teens, and I found myself fighting bouts of severe depression whenever I was alone.

Through unlikely circumstances, I met a young man, and though I liked him from our very first meeting, I had no idea that, in short order, we'd fall madly in love. Given that we were both married, however, it was impossible to pursue the relationship we both badly wanted. Over time, I realized that our secret meetings were getting us nowhere and that something needed to be done if we were to fulfill our dreams.

In the process of formulating a plan, I found myself disregarding everything I knew to be right and proper. Nothing of principle seemed to matter anymore, and I convinced myself that the end justified the means.

On reflection, I'm acutely aware that the passion driving me at the time was nothing short of pure madness.

When I finalized details of the scheme I'd concocted, I knew it likely that the new love of my life may well not go along with it. But that thought only made me more determined to convince him that it was the one and only chance we had.

As I feared, he didn't readily agree to my plan, so I resorted to using the threat of never letting him see me again. While this action on my part didn't immediately persuade him to change his mind, he did agree to us spending a weekend together, in order that we could discuss the matter further. Fortunately, we were able to make this happen by deceiving our respective spouses, which allowed us to spend two nights alone. This gave us the opportunity to talk at length along with several wild, passionate and uninhibited sessions of lovemaking. I'm not sure which of these two foregoing activities had the greatest impact, but on Sunday afternoon, he agreed to go along with my plan.

Funnily enough, though, I now knew that we wouldn't be seeing each other again for nearly two years; it didn't really matter, as every minute of every day, my determination to achieve our goal kept me totally fulfilled.

The next step required me to arrange a ten-year wedding anniversary trip to Wales, and I actually surprised myself at how relatively easy that was to accomplish. Of course, part of my new role depended on rekindling a relationship with Paul, and despite the fact that by now I disliked him intensely, I derived a degree of perverted pleasure from the process of deceiving him. While I'm truly ashamed to say it, I also got some satisfaction from convincing my dear friend Grace that my life with Paul was on the mend! It's no excuse, but at that time, I was totally possessed!

Removing Paul as an obstacle to my future suddenly seemed so inconsequential that I found myself suppressing a morbid desire to laugh when I visualized what I hoped would happen to him later in the year.

Upon our arrival in Wales, I proposed that we celebrate our anniversary eating dinner in the guesthouse restaurant overlooking the lake, knowing this suggestion would almost certainly get unanimous approval. I'd intended to secretly find out what I needed to do in order to get permission to use one of the guest house's rowboats when the time came. This turned out to be a no brainer, as the manager offered this to me without my asking.

I must admit that I wasn't absolutely certain Paul would agree to take me for a boat ride on that infamous Wednesday evening. While I had a backup plan if this became an obstacle, I took steps to increase my odds of success. I was particularly affectionate towards Paul beforehand, and during dinner, I kissed him several times as well. With dinner almost finished, I showered Paul with compliments, refrained from commenting on his drinking, and finally asked him to take me on a romantic trip across the lake. My instincts served me well!

I knew Paul was already quite drunk before we boarded the boat. But for insurance purposes, I suggested he purchase a couple of canned beers to take with us.

Like most men, Paul had certain quirks that, for reasons of ego, he tried to keep a secret. He'd inadvertently revealed one of them to me early in our marriage on a night he was very drunk and most likely had subsequently forgotten doing so. He couldn't swim! While I can't be absolutely certain, I doubt many others knew this. I was sure Grace and Billy didn't, as on the odd occasion the subject was mentioned, Paul's pet line was, "I don't swim unless I have too, but that's only because the water messes up my hair."

Paul's rowing was haphazard, often with the oars missing the water completely, but eventually, we reached a point approximately halfway across the lake. And given that darkness had set in, we were totally out of view from the restaurant. When I asked Paul to stop rowing for a while, I knew he'd take the opportunity to drink the beer he'd brought along. As a backup, I had a whisky miniature in my handbag, which I had intended to give him if I suspected he wasn't drunk enough!

At this juncture, I had several ideas on how to get Paul into the water. Once this was achieved, I knew he'd drown quickly because in his drunken state it would be relatively easy to stop him from climbing back into the boat even if he was sober enough to try.

I waited patiently for Paul to drink the two cans he'd brought with him, and I could tell by his increasingly incoherent speech that he was now completely blotto.

Aware of the potential that the power of suggestion had, I thought I'd try my first line of attack. "Surprised you don't need to urinate after all the beer you've consumed," I called out.

He took the bait. "Definitely could use a piss," came the slurred reply.

Certain, Paul would attempt to stand up in order to open his fly; I offered my assistance. The act of my getting up was sufficient to make the boat rock, and as I helped Paul to his feet, it rocked even more. I was now sure that Paul would be unable to stay upright if I wasn't holding him, so when I removed my support, it came as no surprise that a firm shove in the back sent him flying into the water, whereupon he sank immediately.

I picked up an oar, as I intended to use it to push him back under if he reappeared. But it wasn't necessary. His head did pop up momentarily on one occasion but soon disappeared never to be seen again.

I took my time rowing back to the guest house, trying hard to think how a truly distraught wife would behave in such a situation. I decided to scream as I approached the shore, which had the intended effect. Billy and Grace raced to my aid when they heard me, clearly in a panic. While the two of them helped me out of the boat, I cried hysterically before pre-

tending to faint. It sounds so sinister now, but at the time, I was actually enjoying every moment of my theatrical performance.

The local police carried out an investigation and quickly determined Paul's death to be an accident by misadventure.

Attending Paul's funeral forced me to continue my role as a grieving widow, but again I played it well, spurred on by the knowledge that soon I would be getting an update on the next phase of my plan.

Two months later, a letter was delivered to my house. When I opened it, I took great delight in seeing the note inside was written in the code that I'd devised for the occasion. After going through the decoding process, the message was indeed the one I'd been waiting for.

If everything worked to the schedule I'd set out, I would be receiving another coded message in approximately one year's time! That left one more major task that I needed to accomplish.

Looking forward to the life I hoped lay ahead of me, the months passed quickly, and my spirits remained high.

July finally arrived, as did the letter I'd been waiting patiently for. And given that I'd successfully removed the only other hurdle that could hinder my plan, it was "all systems go!"

Moving to Scotland now only involved a process of making it all appear the result of an unusual and unexpected job opportunity that a grieving widow might easily choose to pursue. And that went forward without a hitch.

When those sitting in judgement of me read the foregoing, there are several other things I'd like them to take into account.

First of all, I'm not asking for mercy or lenience. I will ask that only of my God.

Second, I do beg forgiveness from all members of Paul Weller's family and friends. His death was a hideous and selfish act on my part.

Third, I also beg forgiveness from my family and friends, especially Grace and Billy Andrews and, most of all, my beloved daughter, Sophie. I'd also like to sincerely apologize to those affected, directly and indirectly, by the consequences of every action I took to accomplish my ultimate goals.

 Last, I beg all of you in judgement to know that the acts involved in the process of accomplishing my selfish goals were entirely planned by me and me only. As such, I should and do take full responsibility for them all.

 Shirley Anne Harris (formerly Weller, born Vickers)

 – December 15th, 1963

 The above statement was written by Shirley Harris after being informed by her legal counsel that James Harris had been arrested and charged with being an accomplice to murder.

*   *   *   *

On December 19th, following consultation with her legal counsel, Shirley Harris issued a further statement. It described in detail another hideous crime she had carried out while emphasizing that James Harris had not played an active role in it at any time.

EPILOGUE

Shirley Harris spent a sleepless night in her prison cell; she knew that when dawn broke she would be given her last rights before being escorted to the gallows. Her thoughts focused on the highpoints of her life, those being primarily time spent with her daughter, Sophie, her friend Grace, and James Harris, the only man she had ever loved. She reconciled herself to the fact that while she had only spent a few of her years in a state of married bliss, that time in itself was preferable to spending the rest of life in the misery she had endured during her marriage to Paul.

Since her arrival in Scotland several years prior, Shirley thought it best that James remain nothing more than a name as far as her family or friends were concerned. However, after she married, Grace had asked for a copy of the wedding photograph. While Shirley had been reluctant to send her one, she couldn't find any rationale to deny or ignore such a request, especially coming from her lifelong best friend. Furthermore, she rationalized that the risk of doing so was extremely small, and at the same time, she very much wanted Grace to have a picture of her in a state of euphoria, believing it to be the most beautiful photograph she had ever seen.

Shirley reluctantly came to terms with the fact that she was not being victimized but rather being appropriately punished for a crime she had intentionally committed. Though in spite of this acknowledgement, she couldn't help but see the irony of being caught out in the most unlikely of circumstances. Her best friend,

Grace, had arranged a small party at her home to celebrate her mother-in-law's 70th birthday. In the process, she had asked her husband, Billy, to invite a couple of his mother's closest friends. One of these was a widow named Ada Hoskins, who'd been a school friend of Billy's mother, Vera.

The party had gone off well and was coming to conclusion when Vera asked Grace if she and her friends could see the family photographs that were proudly displayed on the walls of the front parlor. Grace happily accommodated Vera's request and made a point of showing off the photograph of Shirley at her wedding, saying that she and Shirley had been close friends since they were toddlers. In response to a question, Grace explained that Shirley had met her husband through an unlikely job opportunity in Scotland. When asked further about the matter, Grace confirmed that while Shirley's husband was actually born in London, he'd lived all of his adult life in Inverness.

Ada Hoskins had not commented further on Grace's remarks at the time and had decided it best to put the matter to rest, but when she woke up the following morning, the subject was still uppermost in her mind. Her thoughts went back to the time her husband had sadly passed away. To help with her grieving process, she'd taken a part-time job at a local café. She didn't really need the money, but it helped fill in her day. While working there, she often noticed a couple who always sat in the far corner. Though she'd never overheard their conversations, her instincts had told her they were clearly very fond of each other, something that made her happy at the time. But despite Grace's recent emphatic statements to the contrary, Ada was absolutely certain that the couple she'd seen on many occasions were, indeed, Shirley and her husband.

Ada was a thoughtful and clear-minded individual, and not one to act in haste. During the days following the party, Ada found herself chewing over the subject many times. But no matter how hard she tried, she couldn't come up with a logical explanation of what had taken place, and clearly, it wasn't a "slip of the tongue." While Ada was not one to cause trouble, she was, like her late husband, very civic-minded. During a further visit with her friend Vera, she discreetly raised the subject only to find Vera adamantly confirming her daughter-in-law's statements. Though after discussion, Vera changed her mind. On hearing this, she decided it was her duty to report something she found to be very suspicious even though she never expected the matter would be of any particular consequence, let alone lead to a murder investigation. When Shirley Harris saw the unmistakable star-shaped birthmark on Ada Hoskins' hairline following the accidental removal of her wig in the courtroom, she knew beyond any doubt that Ada was indeed the same grey-haired woman who'd served her *Homemade tomato soup* in the café years prior. While Shirley had never mentioned it, this event triggered her full confession, which had the effect she'd intended; namely, charges against her husband were changed from murder to accessory to murder.

At his subsequent trial, James Ralph Harris was sentenced to 12 years imprisonment.

*   *   *   *

Despite total darkness, a vivid image remains imprinted in my mind. It's the most beautiful picture I've ever seen…but how I wish it never existed.